The
Travelling Cat
Chronicles

The
Travelling Cat
Chronicles

HIRO ARIKAWA

Translated from the Japanese
by Philip Gabriel

BERKLEY ∫ NEW YORK

BERKLEY
An imprint of Penguin Random House LLC
375 Hudson Street, New York, New York 10014

Copyright © 2015 by Hiro Arikawa
Translation copyright © 2017 by Philip Gabriel
Penguin Random House supports copyright. Copyright fuels creativity, encourages
diverse voices, promotes free speech, and creates a vibrant culture. Thank you for buying an
authorized edition of this book and for complying with copyright laws by not reproducing,
scanning, or distributing any part of it in any form without permission. You are supporting
writers and allowing Penguin Random House to continue to publish books for every reader.

BERKLEY is a registered trademark and the
B colophon is a trademark of Penguin Random House LLC.

First published in the United Kingdom by Transworld Publishers,
a division of The Random House Group Ltd.

Originally published in Japanese as *Tabineko Ripôto*

Library of Congress Cataloging-in-Publication Data

Names: Arikawa, Hiro, 1972– author. | Gabriel, Philip, 1953– translator.
Title: The travelling cat chronicles / Hiro Arikawa; translated by Philip Gabriel.
Other titles: Tabineko Ripôto. English
Description: New York: Berkley, 2018. | "Originally published
in Japanese as Tabineko Ripôto"—Verso title page. | A reissue of the 2017
edition published by Doubleday (London).
Identifiers: LCCN 2018010823 | ISBN 9780451491336 (hardback) |
ISBN 9780451491343 (ebook)
Subjects: LCSH: Cats—Fiction. | Pets and travel—Fiction. | Human-animal
relationships—Fiction. | Conduct of life—Fiction. | Japan—Fiction. | Domestic fiction. |
BISAC: FICTION / Literary. | FICTION / Family Life. | GSAFD: Road fiction.
Classification: LCC PL867.5.R54 A2 2018 | DDC 895.6/36—dc23
LC record available at https://lccn.loc.gov/2018010823

First Edition: October 2018

Printed in the United States of America
5 7 9 10 8 6

Cover art and design by Adam Auerbach
Text illustrations by Yoco Nagamiya
Title page art: *cat illustration* © Mila Che / Shutterstock.com
Book design by Laura K. Corless

The
Travelling Cat
Chronicles

PROLOGUE

The Cat with No Name

I am a cat. As yet, I have no name. There's a famous cat in our country who once made this very statement.

I have no clue how great that cat was, but at least when it comes to having a name I got there first. Whether I like my name is another matter, since it glaringly doesn't fit my gender, me being male and all. I was given it about five years ago—around the time I came of age.

Back then, I used to sleep on the hood of a silver van in the parking lot of an apartment building. Why there? Because no one would ever shoo me away. Human beings are basically huge monkeys that walk upright, but they can be pretty full of themselves. They leave their cars exposed to the elements, but a few paw prints on the paintwork and they go *ballistic*.

At any rate, the hood of that silver van was my favorite place to sleep. Even in winter, the sun made it all warm and toasty, the perfect spot for a daytime nap.

I stayed there until spring arrived, which meant I'd survived one whole cycle of seasons. One day, I was lying curled up, having a snooze, when I suddenly sensed a warm, intense gaze upon me. I unglued my eyelids a touch and saw a tall, lanky young man, eyes narrowed, staring down at me as I lay prone.

"Do you always sleep there?" he asked.

I suppose so. Do you have a problem with that?

"You're really cute, do you know that?"

So they tell me.

"Is it okay if I stroke you?"

No, thanks. I batted one front paw at him in what I hoped to be a gently threatening way.

"Aren't you a stingy one," the man said, pulling a face.

Well, how would *you* like it if you were sleeping and somebody came by and rubbed you all over?

"I guess you want something in exchange for being stroked?"

Quick on the draw, this one. Quite right. Got to get something in return for having my sleep disturbed. I heard a rustling and popped my head up. The man's hand had disappeared into a plastic bag.

"I don't seem to have bought anything cat-suitable."

No sweat, mate. Feline beggars can't be choosers. That scallop jerky looks tasty.

I sniffed at the package sticking out of the plastic bag and the man, smiling wryly, tapped me on the head with his fingers.

Hey there, let's not jump the gun.

"That's not good for you, cat," he said. "Plus it's too spicy."

Too spicy, says you? Do you think a hungry stray like me

gives a rat's about his health? Getting something into my stomach right this minute—that's my top priority.

At last, the man liberated a slice of fried chicken from a sandwich, stripping off the batter, laying the flesh on his palm and holding it out to me.

You want me to eat right out of your hand? You think you'll get all friendly with me by doing that? I'm not that easy. Then again, it's not often I get to indulge in fresh meat—and it looks kind of succulent—so perhaps a little compromise is in order.

As I chomped down on the chicken, I felt a couple of human fingers slide from under my chin to behind my ears. He scratched me softly. I mean, I'll permit a human who feeds me to touch me for a second, but this guy was pretty clever about it. If he were to give me a couple more tidbits, scratching under my chin would be up for grabs, too. I rubbed my cheek against his hand.

The man smiled, pulled the meat from the second half of the sandwich, stripped off the batter, and held it out. I wanted to tell him I wouldn't say no to the batter, either. It would fill me up even more.

I let him stroke me properly to repay him for the food, but now it was time to close up shop.

Just as I began to raise a front paw and send him on his way, the man said, "Okay, see you later."

He withdrew his hand and walked off, heading up the stairs of the apartment building.

That's how we first met. It wasn't until a little later that he finally gave me my name.

From that moment on, I found crunchy cat food underneath the silver van every night. One human fistful—a full meal for a cat—just behind the rear tire.

If I was around when the man turned up to leave food, he'd wrest some touch-time from me, but when I wasn't there he'd humbly leave an offering and disappear.

Sometimes, another cat would beat me to it, or the man would be away and I'd wait in vain till morning for my crunchies. But, by and large, I could count on him for one square meal a day. Humans are quite flighty, so I don't rely on them a hundred percent. A stray cat's skill lies in building up a complex web of connections in order to survive on the streets.

Acquaintances who understood each other, that's what the man and I had become. But when he and I had settled into a comfortable relationship, fate intervened to change everything.

And fate hurt like hell.

I was crossing the road one night when I became suddenly dazzled by a car's headlights. I was about to dart away when a piercing horn sounded. And that's when it all went wrong. Startled, I was a split second late in leaping aside, and *bang!* the car rammed into me and sent me flying.

I wound up in the bushes by the side of the road. The pain

that shot through my body was like nothing I'd experienced before. But I was alive.

I cursed as I tried to stand up, and even let out a scream. Oww! *Oww!* My right hind leg hurt like you wouldn't believe.

I sank to the ground and twisted my upper half to lick the wound, only to find—good lord! A bone was sticking out!

Bite wounds and cuts I can mostly look after with my tongue, but this was beyond me. Through the wrenching pain, this bone protruding from my leg was making its presence known in no uncertain terms.

What should I do? What *could* I do?

Somebody, help me! But that was idiotic. Nobody was going to help a stray.

Then I remembered the man who came every night to leave me crunchies. Maybe he could help.

Why this thought came to me, I don't know—we'd always kept our distance, with occasional stroking time in thanks for his offerings. But it was worth a try.

I set off along the pavement, dragging my right hind leg with the bone jabbing out. Several times my body gave out, as if to say, *I can't take it, it's just too painful. Not one. More. Step.*

By the time I reached the silver van, dawn was breaking.

I really couldn't take another step. This is it, I thought.

I cried out at the top of my lungs.

Oww ... owwwww!

Again and again I screamed, until my voice finally gave out. It killed me even to call out, to be honest with you.

Just then, I heard someone come down the stairs of the apartment building. When I looked up, I saw it was the man.

"I *thought* it was you."

When he saw me close up, he turned pale.

"What happened? Were you hit by a car?"

Hate to admit it, but I messed up.

"Does it hurt? It looks like it."

Enough of the irritating questions. Have a little pity for a wounded cat, okay?

"It sounded like you were desperate, the way you were screaming, and it woke me up. You were calling for me, weren't you, cat?"

Yes, yes, I certainly was! But you took your time getting here.

"You thought I might be able to help you, didn't you?"

I guess so, Sherlock. Then the man started sniffing and snuffling. Why was *he* crying?

"I'm proud of you, remembering me like that."

Cats don't cry like humans do. But—somehow—I sort of understood why he was weeping.

So you'll do something to help, won't you? I can't stand the pain much longer.

"There, there. You'll be okay, cat."

The man laid me gently in a cardboard box lined with a fluffy towel and placed me in the front seat of the silver van.

We headed for the vet's clinic. That's like the worst place ever for me, so I'd rather not talk about it.

I ended up staying with the man until my wounds healed. He lived alone in his apartment and everything was neat and tidy. He set out a litter tray for me in the changing area beside the bath, and bowls of food and water in the kitchen.

Despite appearances, I'm a pretty intelligent, well-mannered cat, and I worked out how to use the toilet right away and never once soiled the floor. Tell me not to sharpen my claws on certain places, and I refrain. The walls and door frames were forbidden so I used the furniture and rug for claw-sharpening. I mean, he never specifically mentioned that the furniture and the rug were off limits. (Admittedly, he did look a little put out at first, but I'm the kind of cat who can pick up on things, sniff out what's absolutely forbidden, and what isn't. The furniture and the rug weren't *absolutely* off limits, is what I'm saying.)

I think it took about two months to get the stitches out and for the bone to heal. During that time, I found out the man's name. Satoru Miyawaki.

Satoru kept calling me things like "You," or "Cat" or "Mr. Cat"—whatever he felt like at the time. Which is understandable, since I didn't have a name at this point.

And even if I *had* had a name, Satoru didn't understand my language, so I wouldn't have been able to tell him. It's kind of inconvenient that humans only understand each other. Did you know that animals are much more multilingual?

Whenever I wanted to go outside, Satoru would frown and try to convince me that I shouldn't.

"If you go out, you might never come back. Just be patient, little cat. Wait until you're completely better. You don't want to have stitches in your leg for the rest of your life, do you?"

By this time, I was able to walk a little, though it still hurt, but seeing how put out Satoru looked, I endured house confinement for those two months, and I figured there were benefits. It wouldn't do to be dragging my leg if a rival cat and I got into a scrap.

So I stayed put until my wound was at long last totally healed.

Satoru always used to stop me at the front door with a worried look, but now I stood there, meowing to be let out. Thank you for all you've done. I will be forever grateful. I wish you lifelong happiness, even if you never leave me another tidbit beneath that silver van.

Satoru didn't look worried so much as forlorn. The same way he seemed about the furniture and the rug. It's not totally off limits, but still … *That* sort of expression.

"Do you still prefer to live outside?"

Hang on now—enough with the teary face. You look like that, you'll start making *me* feel sad that I'm leaving.

And then, out of the blue: "Listen, Cat, I was wondering if you would become my cat."

I had never considered this as an option. Being a dyed-in-the-wool stray, the thought of being someone's pet had never crossed my mind.

My idea was to let him look after me until I recovered, but I'd always planned to leave once my wound was healed. Let me rephrase that. I thought I *had* to leave.

As long as I was leaving, it would be a lot more dignified to slip out on my own rather than have someone shoo me away. Cats are proud creatures, after all.

If you wanted me to be your pet cat, then, well, you should have said so earlier.

I slipped out of the door that Satoru had reluctantly opened. Then I turned around and gave him a meow.

Come on.

For a human, Satoru had a good intuitive sense of cat language and seemed to understand what I was saying. He looked puzzled for a moment, then followed me outside.

It was a bright, moonlit night, and the town lay still and quiet.

I leaped onto the hood of the silver van, thrilled to have regained the ability to jump, and then back onto the ground, where I rolled and scratched for a bit.

A car drove by and my tail shot up, the fear of being hit again ingrained in me now. Before I knew it, I was hiding behind Satoru's trousered legs, and he was gazing down at me, smiling.

I made one round of the neighborhood with Satoru before returning to the apartment building. Outside the door of the stairway to the apartment on the second floor, I meowed. Open up.

I looked up at Satoru and saw he was smiling, but again in that tearful way.

"So you *do* want to come back, eh, Mr. Cat?"

Right. Yeah. So open up.

"So you'll be my cat?"

Okay. But sometimes let's go out for a walk.

And so I became Satoru's cat.

When I was a child, I had a cat that looked just like you." Satoru brought a photo album out of the cupboard. "See?"

The album was full of photos of a cat. I know what they call people like this. *Cat fanatics.*

The cat in the photos did indeed resemble me. Both of us had an almost all-white body, the only spots of color being on our face and tail. Two on our face; our tails black and bent. The only difference was in the angle of our bent tails. The tabby spots on our faces, though, were exactly alike.

"The two spots on its forehead were angled downwards, like the Chinese character *hachi*—eight—so I named him Hachi."

If that's how he comes up with names, what on earth is he going to choose for me?

After *hachi* comes *kyu*—nine. What if he picked that?

"How about Nana?"

What? He's subtracting? I didn't see that coming.

"It hooks in the opposite direction from Hachi's, and from the top it looks like *nana*—the number seven."

He seemed to be talking about my tail now.

Now wait just a second. Isn't Nana a girl's name? I'm a fully fledged, hot-blooded male. In what universe does that make sense?

"You're okay with that, aren't you, Nana? It's a lucky name—Lucky Seven and all that."

I meowed, and Satoru squinted and tickled me under my chin.

"Do you like the name?"

Nope! But, well. Asking that while stroking my chin is playing foul. I purred in spite of myself.

"So you like it. Great."

I told you already—*I do not.*

In the end, I missed my chance to undo the mistake (I mean, what's a cat going to do? The guy was petting me the whole time), and that's how I ended up being Nana.

"We'll have to move, won't we?"

His landlord didn't allow pets in the apartment, but he'd made an exception for me, just until I got back on my paws.

So Satoru moved with me to a new place in the same town. Going to all that trouble to move just for the sake of one cat—well, maybe I shouldn't say this, being a cat myself, but that was one fired-up cat lover.

And so began our new life together. Satoru was the perfect

roommate for a cat, and I was the perfect roommate for a human.

We've got along really well, these past five years.

ও

As a cat, I was now in the prime of life, and as Satoru was a little over thirty, I guess he was, too.

One day, Satoru patted my head apologetically.

"Nana, I'm sorry."

It's okay, it's okay. No worries.

"I'm really sorry it's come to this."

No need to explain. I'm quick on the uptake.

"I never intended to let you go."

Life, be it human or feline, doesn't always work out the way you think it will.

If I had to give up living with Satoru, I'd just go back to the way I was five years ago. Back when the bone was sticking out of my leg. If we'd said good-bye and I'd gone back to life on the streets, it would not have been a big deal. I could go back to being a stray tomorrow, no problem.

I wouldn't have lost anything. Just gained the name Nana, and the five years I'd spent with Satoru.

So don't look so glum, chum.

Cats just quietly take whatever comes their way.

The only exception so far was the night I broke my leg and thought of Satoru.

"Well, shall we go?"

It seemed Satoru wanted me to go with him somewhere. He opened the door of my basket and I got in without making a fuss. For the five years I'd lived with him, I'd always been a sensible cat. For instance, even when he took me to my bête noire, the vet, I didn't make a racket.

Okay then—let's go. As Satoru's roommate, I had been a perfect cat, so I should be the perfect companion on this journey he seemed so intent on making.

My basket in hand, Satoru got into the silver van.

1

The Husband without a Wife

L *ong time no see.*
    So began the e-mail.

It was from Satoru Miyawaki, a childhood friend of Kosuke's who had moved away when he was in elementary school. He had moved around quite a bit after that, but they never completely lost touch, and even now, when they were both past thirty, they were still friends.

Sorry this is out of the blue, but would you be able to take my cat for me?

It was his precious cat, which "unavoidable circumstances" were preventing him from keeping any longer, and he was now looking for someone to take care of it.

What these unavoidable circumstances were, he didn't say.

He'd attached two photos. A cat with two spots on his forehead forming the character *hachi*—eight.

"Whoa!" Kosuke couldn't help saying. "This cat looks exactly like Hachi."

The cat in the photo looked just like the one Satoru and Kosuke had found that day so many years ago.

Kosuke scrolled to a second photo, a close-up of the cat's tail. A hooked tail like the number seven.

Aren't cats with hooked tails supposed to bring good fortune? thought Kosuke.

He tried to recall who had told him that. Then he sighed, realizing it had been his wife, who'd gone to live with her parents for a while. Kosuke had no clue when she'd be back.

He was beginning to get the faint sense that maybe she never would.

The ridiculous thought crossed his mind that perhaps if they'd had a cat like this, things might have been different.

With a cat hanging around the house, a cat with a hooked tail to gather in pieces of happiness, maybe they'd be able to live a simpler, more innocent life. Even without any children.

Might be good to have the cat, he was thinking. The cat in the photo was good-looking, a lot like Hachi, with the hooked tail and everything. And he hadn't seen Satoru for a long time.

A friend asked me to take his cat for him, so what do you think? Kosuke e-mailed his wife, and she answered: *Do whatever you like.* A tad cold, he thought, but since she hadn't replied to a single e-mail since she'd left, it felt good to hear from her, at least.

He began to wonder if his wife, a true cat lover, might actually come home if he took in the cat. Perhaps if he told her he had adopted the animal but didn't know how to look after it and begged her to help, perhaps she would come back solely out of sympathy for the cat.

No. Dad hates cats, so that won't work. He caught his own

knee-jerk reaction; he was worrying, as usual, about what his father might think.

This was exactly why his wife had got fed up with him. Kosuke was the one running the business now, and there was no need to worry about how his dad would feel about things. Yet still he did.

So, partly as a reaction against his dad, he threw his name—Kosuke Sawada—into the ring as a candidate willing to take in his childhood friend's cat.

Satoru wasted no time coming over to Kosuke's place, arriving on Kosuke's day off the following week in his silver van, along with his beloved cat.

When he heard a car engine outside his shop, Kosuke wandered out to find Satoru pulling into the shop's parking lot.

"Kosuke! It's been ages!"

Satoru took his hands off the wheel and waved out of the open driver's-side window.

"Just hurry up and park," Kosuke urged. He was excited to see Satoru. The guy hadn't changed at all since he was a kid.

"You should have parked at the end. It's easier."

There were three parking spaces for customers right in front of the shop and Satoru had pulled into the spot furthest from the entrance, where a small shed and piles of boxes made it a tight fit.

"Ah, is that right?" Satoru said, scratching his head as he

got out of the van. "I didn't want to take up a space in case a customer needed it. Well, it's done now." He took the cat basket from the backseat.

"Is that Nana?"

"Yep. I sent you a photo so you could see how his tail is shaped like a seven. Great name, don't you think?"

"I don't know if I'd call it great, exactly ... You always choose kind of quirky names ... Like Hachi."

Kosuke ushered them into his living room and tried to get a good look at Nana's face, but all Nana did was give a moody growl and turn himself around. When Kosuke peered inside the basket, all he could make out was the black hooked tail and white rear end.

"What's the matter, Nana? Nana-chan ... ?"

Satoru tried to coax Nana out, but eventually gave up.

"Sorry about that. He must be nervous about being in a different house. Give it some time and I'm sure he'll settle down ..."

They left the basket door open and sat on the sofa together to reminisce over old times.

"You're driving, so alcohol's no good. What would you like to drink? Coffee? Tea?"

Kosuke brewed two cups of coffee. Satoru took his carefully and asked, innocently enough, "Is your wife here today?"

Kosuke had intended to avoid the issue but, after an awkward silence, failed to come up with a plausible excuse.

"She went back to her parents' place."

"Oh …"

Satoru's face was hard to describe. A *sorry I didn't realize that was such a sore point* kind of look.

"Is it okay for you to make a decision about the cat on your own? Won't you two quarrel about it when she comes home?"

"She likes cats. In fact, taking the cat might lure her back."

"Yeah, but not everybody likes the same type of cat."

"I forwarded those photos of Nana to her and asked her what she thought, and she said I should do whatever I like."

"That doesn't sound like she's on board with the idea."

"It's the only time since she left that she's answered one of my e-mails."

Taking the cat might lure her back—Kosuke had said it as a joke, but he was actually hoping it might be true.

"She's not the type of woman to chuck out a cat. And if she never comes home, then I'll look after it myself. Either way, I don't see any problem."

"I see," Satoru said, backing down. Now it was Kosuke's turn to ask the questions.

"But tell me, why can't you keep the cat anymore?"

"Well, it's just that …"

Satoru gave a perplexed smile and scratched at the thinning hair on his head.

"Something came up, and we can't live together anymore."

Something clicked. Kosuke had known something was awry when Satoru, who had a nine-to-five job, had offered to work around Kosuke's day off and come over in the middle of the week.

"Have you been laid off?"

"Not exactly, well—in any case, we just can't live together anymore."

Kosuke didn't pursue it, since Satoru seemed reluctant to talk about it.

"Anyhow, I've got to find a home for Nana, and I've asked a couple of friends."

"I see. That can't be easy."

It made Kosuke want to take the cat even more. As an act of kindness. And besides, it was for Satoru.

"What about *you*? Are you okay? Your—plans for the future, and everything?"

"Thanks for asking. As long as I can get Nana settled, I'll be fine."

Kosuke sensed he shouldn't probe any further. Resisted the *if there's anything I can do, let me know* line.

"You know, when I saw the photo, I was amazed. Nana's the spitting image of Hachi."

"Even more so when you see him in the flesh."

Satoru glanced back at the basket still sitting on the floor, but it didn't look like Nana was intending to show his face anytime soon.

"When I first saw him, I was surprised, too. For a second I thought it *was* Hachi."

That was impossible, of course, but the memory saddened him, nonetheless. "What happened to Hachi?" Kosuke asked.

"He died when I was in high school. His new owner got in touch, told me it was a traffic accident."

Even now, this must have been a painful memory for Satoru.

"It's nice that they let you know, though."

At least the two of them, who had both loved the cat, could mourn together. Satoru must have cried alone many times since.

"Sorry, I seem to be getting sadder and sadder here," Satoru said.

"Don't apologize, you idiot."

Kosuke made as if to lightly punch him and Satoru playfully swayed to avoid it.

"Time goes by before you know it," Satoru said. "It seems like yesterday when you and I found Hachi. Do you remember?"

"Remember? How could I forget?" Kosuke smiled, and Satoru gave a little embarrassed *ahem* laugh.

∽

A short walk from the Sawada Photo Studio, up a gentle slope, was a housing complex. Twenty-five years ago, this was considered an up-and-coming area, with rows of model showroom-like houses and fashionable condo units.

Satoru's family lived in a cozy condo in the neighborhood. Satoru and his parents: the three of them.

Satoru and Kosuke had started going to the same swimming club in second grade. Since he was little, Kosuke had struggled with skin allergies, and his mother, convinced that swimming would make his skin tougher, had made him go, but Satoru had a different reason for going. He was such a fast swimmer people said he had webbed hands, and the teachers at his school had recommended he learn to swim properly.

Always a bit of a joker, Satoru, when they had free swimming time, would pretend to be a salamander and crawl along the bottom of the pool, then playfully pop up and pounce on the other pupils. "What are you, some kind of *kappa*?" the swimming instructor had said, irritated, and the nickname Kappa—a kind of mythical water imp—stuck. Depending on the instructor's mood, he sometimes called him Webfoot, too.

Once lessons began, though, Satoru was in the advanced class for kids who could swim fast, while Kosuke was in the ordinary class that included all the kids like him with allergies.

Despite all the Kappa and Webfoot antics, when Satoru swam at speed down the lane he looked incredibly cool. Kosuke and Satoru were good friends, but at those times Kosuke found Satoru a little annoying. *If only I could be like him*, he thought enviously.

But one day he saw Satoru clowning around, diving into

the water and cracking his forehead on the bottom, and he was no longer so envious.

It was early summer, and they had been going to the swimming club for two years.

They always met up at the bottom of the slope below the housing complex to walk to swimming club together, and on this day Kosuke was the first to arrive. Which is why he was the one to discover the box first.

A cardboard box had been left below the post with the map of the housing complex on it. And the box was meowing. Hesitantly, Kosuke opened the lid and saw two white balls of downy fur. With a sprinkling of tabby patches here and there.

He stared silently at them. Such helpless, soft little things, he thought. They were so tiny he hesitated even to touch them—

"Wow! Cats!"

From above him, Satoru's voice rang out.

"What's up?" he said, crouching down beside Kosuke.

"Somebody just left it here."

"They're so cute!"

In silence, the two boys timidly stroked the fluffy fur for a few moments, then Satoru spoke.

"Do you want to hold him?"

You have allergies, so don't ever touch animals—Kosuke could hear his mother's scolding voice in his head, but he couldn't just stand and watch Satoru give them a stroke. Kosuke had been the one to find them, after all.

He scooped one of them up in his hands and placed it on his palm. It was so light!

He wanted to carry on stroking them, but they were going to be late for swimming. Reluctantly, they peeled the kittens off them and returned them to the box.

They agreed that they would look in on the kittens on the way back, and raced down the road to the swimming club. They were a few minutes late for class and the instructor slapped them both on the head.

After class, they fell over themselves to get back to the bottom of the slope below the housing complex.

The box was still there, under the sign, but to their dismay, now there was only one kitten inside. Someone must have taken the other one.

It seemed to them that the fate of the remaining kitten lay in their hands. A kitten with tabby patches on its forehead in the shape of the character *hachi*. And a black hooked tail.

The two of them sat down on the grass beside the box and gazed at the little kitten curled up in it, sleeping soundly. How could any child not want to take this tiny, soft little creature home?

What would happen if we did take it home? Each boy knew exactly what the other was thinking.

Kosuke knew his mom would be against it because of his allergies, plus his dad wasn't so keen on animals.

In contrast to Kosuke, Satoru was quick to come to a decision.

"I'll ask my mom."

"That's not fair!"

Kosuke's reaction was fueled by something that had happened at swimming club a few days before. A girl Kosuke was keen on saw Satoru swimming in the advanced class and murmured, "He's pretty cool."

Satoru could swim fast, he didn't have any allergies, and his father and mother were both kind people, so if he took the cat home they were sure to accept it. So not only did the girl Kosuke liked praise Satoru, but now he would get to keep this soft, tiny creature—that just wasn't fair, was it?

When Kosuke told him this, Satoru looked hurt, as if he'd been slapped. Kosuke felt ashamed.

He'd simply been getting something off his chest, that was all.

"I mean, I found him first," he finally blurted out.

To which Satoru, honest to a fault, said, "I'm sorry. Yes, you did find him first, Kosuke, so he's your cat."

Kosuke regretted having snapped at his friend, but all he could manage was a small nod. They parted a little awkwardly, and Kosuke carried the cardboard box with the kitten inside it home.

His mother, surprisingly, wasn't against keeping the kitten.

"Perhaps it's because of the swimming, but you haven't had any allergic reactions lately, so as long as we keep the house really clean, I think it should be okay."

The main obstacle was his father.

"No way! A *cat*? Are you insane?"

That was his immediate reaction, and he refused to change his mind.

"What if he scratches everything with his claws? Looking after a cat costs money, you know! I'm not running a photo studio to feed some cat!"

Kosuke's mother supported her son, but that seemed to make his father even more resistant to the idea. Before they had dinner, he ordered Kosuke to take the cat back where he'd found it.

So Kosuke, on the verge of tears, trudged back to the slope below the housing complex with the cardboard box held tightly to his chest.

But put the box back under the sign? He couldn't bring himself to do that. And so he found himself heading for his friend's house.

My dad said I can't keep the cat." Standing at the door sobbing, Kosuke finally managed to get the words out.

"I get it," Satoru said, and nodded. "Leave it to me. I have a great idea!"

Satoru disappeared inside the house. Kosuke waited at the door, guessing that he was going to ask his mother if he could keep the cat, but then Satoru reappeared, with his swimming bag slung across his shoulder.

"Satoru, where are you going with that?" his mother called

out from the kitchen. "We're going to have dinner as soon as your father gets home!"

"You go ahead and eat!" Satoru called out, slipping into his sneakers at the entrance. "Kosuke and I are going to run away from home for a while!"

"*What?*"

Satoru's mother was always so graceful and gentle. Kosuke had never heard her sound so stern.

She seemed to be in the middle of deep-frying tempura, so although she wasn't happy about it, she couldn't come to the front door. Instead, she just popped her head out from the kitchen.

"Ko-chan, what is he talking about?" she asked.

But Kosuke was equally clueless.

"Come on," Satoru said. He pulled Kosuke by the hand and they ran out of the house.

"I read this book at school the other day," Satoru explained. "A boy found a stray puppy and his father got angry and told him to take it back where he had found it, but he couldn't bring himself to do it so he ran away from home. In the middle of the night, his father came looking for him and, in the end, he said he would let him keep it, as long as he looked after it himself."

Satoru rattled on excitedly.

"What we're doing is exactly the same, Kosuke, so I'm sure it'll work out! The only difference is it's a stray cat, not a dog. And you have me to help you."

Apart from it being a kitten, not a puppy, Kosuke had the feeling that his situation was quite different from the one in the book, though he was, admittedly, quite attracted by the idea of his father feeling sad and giving in if he ran away.

He decided to go along with the plan. The first thing they did was go to a small supermarket and buy some cat food. "We'd like food for a kitten," they told the man at the cash register, and the man, whose hair was dyed red, said, "Try this," and handed them a can of paste-like meat. The man had looked intimidating at first but turned out to be unexpectedly kind.

Then they had dinner in the park of the housing complex. Satoru had grabbed some bread and sweets from his house, and the two of them made do with that. They opened the can of cat food for the kitten.

"So, by 'middle of the night,' I'm guessing we need to hang out here until about twelve."

Satoru had prudently packed an alarm clock in his bag.

"But won't my father have a total fit if I stay out that late?"

Kosuke's father seemed friendly enough outside the house, but with his family he was an obstinate man with a short fuse.

"What are you talking about? We're doing it for the cat, aren't we? And besides, he'll forgive you in the end, so it'll all work out."

In the book, the father had forgiven his son, but caught up in Satoru's blind enthusiasm, Kosuke didn't feel able to say what was on his mind, namely that his father had a very different personality, and he doubted that the plan would succeed.

As they whiled away the time playing with the cat in the park, a few people, out for a stroll, called out to them, among them a woman walking her dogs.

"What are you doing out this late? Your family will be worried," she said.

They were too well known in the neighborhood. Kosuke started to wonder if they'd chosen the wrong spot, though Satoru didn't seem at all concerned.

"Don't worry about us," he told the woman. "We're running away!"

"Is that so? Well, you'd better go home right now!"

After a fifth woman had come up to them, Kosuke finally raised an objection.

"Satoru, I don't think this is how you run away from home."

"I know, but in the book the father came looking for them in a park."

"Yeah, but this doesn't make any sense."

At that moment, they heard a voice calling through the cool air: "Satoru!" It was his mother. "It's late, and enough is enough. Come home now! You've got Kosuke's family worried, too!"

Satoru flinched. "There's no way they could have found us so quickly!"

"You didn't think they'd find us?"

Had Satoru seriously believed they could hide from their parents when there were all these strangers around who seemed to know them?

"I'm sorry, Mom!" Satoru shouted. "But we can't be found yet!

"Come on, Kosuke!" He grabbed the cardboard box and ran with it to the gate leading out of the park. Kosuke could do nothing but follow. It felt like they were straying from the storyline Satoru had described, but there should still be time to put that right. Surely there would be. Well, maybe.

They managed to shake off Satoru's mother and were sprinting down the slope away from the housing complex when all of a sudden there was a roar.

"Come back here!"

The roar came from Kosuke's father. It was probably too late now to put anything right. Maybe we should just apologize, Kosuke was thinking, but Satoru shouted: "It's the enemy!"

The story had taken a different turn now.

"Run for it!"

By now, they'd completely lost sight of the narrative they were supposed to be sticking to. For the time being, all Kosuke could do was chase after Satoru, who was determined to keep running.

His portly and generally sedentary father couldn't keep up and they lost him after they'd rounded the first corner, but now the street was totally straight. There was nowhere to hide.

"Kosuke, this way!"

Satoru had raced inside the small supermarket where they'd bought the can of cat food. A smattering of customers were flipping through magazines while the red-haired clerk listlessly restocked a shelf.

"You have to hide us! We're being chased!" Satoru shouted. The clerk looked over at them doubtfully.

"If they catch us, they're going to get rid of him!"

Satoru showed the cardboard box to the clerk and a siren-like yowl rang out from it.

The clerk stared at the box for a moment, then headed to the back of the shop, motioning for them to follow. They passed through a door and the clerk pointed to the back exit.

"You're a lifesaver!"

Satoru scampered out, followed by Kosuke.

He turned and gave a small bow of thanks, and the clerk wordlessly waved a hand at them.

From there, they scurried from place to place, but they were only children and there was only so far their legs could carry them.

Finally, they ran to their elementary school. Satoru's odd little plan to run away from home had caused quite a disturbance, so much so that the news had got around the neighborhood, and as they legged it into the school grounds, all the grown-ups were hot on their heels.

They prized open a window, one that all the pupils knew was out of kilter and didn't lock properly, and slipped into the school building. The adults had no idea how to get in, so they ran around helplessly outside, while the boys made their way up to the top floor.

They spilled out onto the roof and could at last put down the cardboard box with the kitten inside.

"I hope he's okay. He was quite shaken up."

There was no sound coming from the box so they quickly opened it. The kitten was nestled in a corner. Kosuke hesitantly reached his arm inside to touch it—

Pyaaa—!

The kitten started to howl even louder than before.

"Sssshhhh! You'll give us away."

The two boys tried to calm the kitten, but cats don't often listen. Crouched down and shushing at each other, they could hear voices calling out.

"I hear a cat!"

"It's coming from the roof!"

The grown-ups had started to gather down below.

"Kosuke, enough!"

One angry voice rose up from the crowd, that of Kosuke's father. From his tone, it was easy to guess that his son was in for a beating.

Kosuke, in tears, turned on Satoru.

"It didn't work! You lied, Satoru!"

"It isn't over yet. We can still pull this off!"

Again, a voice called out from below. "Satoru, come down here right this minute!"

Satoru's father had joined their pursuers.

"We can go up the fire escape," someone piped up, and it

became clear that Kosuke's father, his face burning with rage, was already climbing the stairs.

"It's all over now," Kosuke mumbled, holding his head in his hands. Satoru ran over to the railing on the roof. He leaned over it and shouted, "Stop! If you don't stop, he's going to jump!"

A murmur ran through the crowd below.

"*What?*" Kosuke was horrified. "What are you doing, Satoru?!"

When he grabbed Satoru's sleeve, Satoru gave him a blazing grin and a thumbs-up. "A comeback!" he said. It wasn't what Kosuke had been hoping for, but it did seem to be enough to stop Kosuke's father dead in his tracks.

"Satoru, is that true, what you said?" Satoru's mother yelled from below.

"It's true! It's true!" Satoru yelled back. "He just took off his sneakers!"

"Oh my god!" People were screaming from below.

"Kosuke, calm down now, kid!" This from Satoru's father, while Kosuke's father roared, "Stop buggering about!" Even from up above, it was clear he was furious. "Stop whining! I'm coming up, and I'll drag you down from there if I have to!"

"Don't do that, Mr. Sawada! Kosuke's really going to do it!" Satoru shouted, to stop him. "If you come up here, he'll jump off, and he'll take the cat with him!"

Satoru turned to Kosuke with a grave expression on his face. "Kosuke, could you, like, kind of straddle the railing?"

Kosuke replied that no way was he going to risk his life over all this.

"But look, you want to keep the cat, don't you?"

"Sure, but ..." For the sake of a cat, did you really have to go this far?

For one thing, the story Satoru had read about the boy running away hadn't ended up with him and the puppy jumping to their deaths.

"Listen! Can't we ask first whether it's okay to keep the cat at your house, Satoru?"

"What?" Satoru looked as startled as a pigeon shot with an air rifle. "You mean, it's okay for *me* to have the cat? Man, if you thought that, you should have said so!"

Beaming, Satoru called out to the crowd down below.

"Dad! Mom! Kosuke says he wants us to have the cat—!"

"Okay, okay. But first talk Kosuke out of jumping!"

A storm of misunderstanding still seemed to be swirling through the crowd of grown-ups, who didn't have a clue what was going on.

၏

Satoru, you really weren't too bright as a child, were you?

I could hear Satoru and Kosuke's conversation from inside my basket. I'd never heard such a mad story in my life.

"It was after we came down from the roof that things got heavy."

"Your dad thumped us pretty hard, Kosuke. I remember, the next day my head looked like the Great Buddha in Nara."

The cat that had thrown the whole neighborhood into such an uproar was my predecessor, that cat Hachi, apparently.

"Speaking of which, Hachi was a male tabby, wasn't he? Aren't male tabbies supposed to be quite rare?" asked Kosuke.

Is that so? Well, since Hachi and I have the same markings, I must be a pretty rare specimen myself.

I had pricked up my ears to listen in, and Satoru said, smiling, "Well, the thing is ... I asked a vet about it and he said his markings are too few for him to be classified as a tabby."

"Really? Other than his forehead and tail, it's true—he was pure white."

Kosuke paused. "Man," he said, raising his arms then crossing them in front of his chest. I could see all this through the gaps in my basket. "I was thinking that if I had told my father it was a valuable male tabby I might have been able to convince him to keep it."

Kosuke looked over at the basket. I quickly turned my head away so as not to meet his eye. Too much bother if he tries to get all friendly on me.

"What about Nana? His face looks exactly like Hachi's, but what about his markings?"

"Nana can't be classified as a tabby either. He's just a mutt."

Well, *excuuuse me.* I glared at the back of Satoru's head, and he went on:

"But, to me, Nana's much more valuable than a male tabby. It's fate, don't you think, that he looks just like the first cat I ever had? When I first laid eyes on him, I knew, someday, he had to be my own precious cat."

Harrumph. You're just saying that because it sounds good. I know what you're getting at. But still.

Maybe that's why I saw Satoru crying that day. After I was hit by the car and had dragged myself back to his place. He mentioned that Hachi had died in a traffic accident.

Satoru must have thought he was going to lose another precious cat to a car accident.

"That was one good cat, Hachi. So well behaved," Kosuke said.

To which Satoru replied, with a smile, "Though he wasn't very athletic."

According to what I heard, he was the type whose legs went all spongy when someone grabbed the back of his neck. A cat who couldn't catch mice, in other words. Pretty pathetic, if you ask me. A real cat would immediately fold in its legs.

Me? I'm a real cat, naturally. I caught my first sparrow when I was less than six months old. And catching something with wings is a lot trickier than catching any four-legged land creature, believe you me.

"When he was playing with a catnip toy he'd go dizzy, chasing it around."

"'Cause he was usually pretty placid."

"What about Nana?"

"He loves mouse toys. The kind made out of rabbit fur."

Hold on a sec. I can't let that pass. Since when did I *love* that awful fake mouse?

It smells like the real thing, so if you throw it near me, of course I'll fight with it, but no matter how much I chomp on it, no tasty juice comes out. So when I finally calm down I'm worn out, and the whole thing's been a total waste of time, d'you understand?

There's that manga on TV sometimes where the samurai cuts down a dingbat and sighs, "That was a waste of a good sword." To me, that's kind of how it feels. You've hunted down yet another useless thing. (By the way, Satoru prefers the shows with guns.) The least they could do would be to stuff those toys with white meat. But could I take this complaint to the pet-toymakers? Stop worrying about what the owners think and pay some attention to your real clients. Your *real* clients are folk like *me*.

In any case, after one of those pointless chases, I usually let off steam with a good walk. But Satoru usually tags along, and that makes it hard to do any successful hunting.

What I mean is, the minute I spot some decent game, Satoru interferes. Deliberately makes some careless noise or movement. When I glare at him, he feigns ignorance, but all that racket gives us away, thank you very much.

When I get upset and wave my tail energetically from side to side, he gives me this pathetic look and tries to explain.

You have lots of crunchies at home to eat, don't you? You

don't need to kill anything. Even if you catch something, Nana, you barely eat it.

You idiot, idiot, idioooooottttt! Every living creature on earth is born with an instinct to kill! You can try to dodge it by bringing in vegetarianism, but you just don't hear a plant scream when you kill it! Hunting down what can be hunted is a cat's natural instinct! Sometimes we hunt things but don't eat them, but that's what training is all about.

My god, what spineless creatures they are, those that don't kill the food they eat. Satoru's a human being, of course, so he just doesn't get it.

"Is Nana good at hunting?"

"He's beyond good! He caught a pigeon that landed on our porch."

Right you are. Those blasted birds get all superior in human territory. I thought I'd show them what's what. And Satoru, all teary-eyed, always asked, "Why do you catch them if you're not going to eat them?" If that's the way you think, then don't interfere when I hunt on our walks.

And didn't Satoru complain about pigeon droppings on the laundry he'd hung out to dry? He'd be happy if I chased away the pigeons, and I'd get to hunt. Literally, two birds with one stone, so why the complaints? And by the by, ever since that incident, the pigeons have never come near our porch again, but have I heard a word of thanks? Still waiting!

"It was a real problem that time," Satoru said. "A sparrow or a mouse I could bury in the bushes next to the apartment building, but something the size of a pigeon, that's a different story. I ended up burying it in a park, and the only conclusion anybody who spotted me, a thirty-year-old man burying a pigeon, could come to is that I was a pretty dodgy character."

"There are more and more weird things happening these days, too."

"Right. Every time someone passed by, I would say apologetically, 'I'm so sorry, but the cat did it,' and they'd look at me really oddly. And wouldn't you know it, that was the one occasion Nana wasn't with me."

Ah, so he had an awkward time, did he? I should have been with him. But Satoru didn't tell me, so it's *his* fault, and I'm not going to apologize.

"Sounds like Nana's wilder than Hachi was."

"But he's quite gentle sometimes, too, like Hachi. When I'm feeling depressed or down, he always snuggles up close . . ."

Not that hearing these words made me happy or anything.

"Sometimes, I get the feeling he can understand what people are saying. He's pretty bright."

Humans who think we *don't* understand them are the stupid ones.

"Hachi was a very kind cat. Whenever my father had a go at me and I went to your house, Satoru, he'd sit on my lap and refuse to jump off."

"He understood when people were feeling down. When my parents had an argument, he'd always side with the one who had lost. It made it easy for me as a child to tell who had won and who had lost."

"I wonder if Nana would do the same, too?"

"I'm sure of it. He's pretty kind."

Hachi seemed to be a decent sort of cat, but going on and on about *Hachi this* and *Hachi that* made me think, *If a cat that's dead was so good, maybe I should die, too, and let them see how they like that.*

"I'm sorry," Kosuke suddenly murmured. "I should have taken Hachi from you back then."

"There was nothing we could do about it."

Satoru sounded like he didn't hold a grudge. Instead, looking at Kosuke, it seemed to me that he was the one who did.

∽

Though Satoru's family brought Hachi up, it was as though Kosuke did the job half the time.

Whenever he went over to Satoru's, he played tirelessly with Hachi, and Satoru sometimes took the cat over to Kosuke's house.

At first, Kosuke's father stubbornly refused to let Hachi in the house, so they played in the garage, but before long his mother let them bring the cat inside, if not into the studio, and little by little his father got used to it. He warned them not to let Hachi sharpen his claws on the walls or the furniture, but sometimes, when he passed by, Kosuke's father would say a few nice things to Hachi.

Kosuke regretted that he couldn't have Hachi himself, but he was very happy when his father played with him. It felt like his father was meeting him halfway. He even hoped that, if he ever found another stray kitten, this time he would be allowed to keep it for himself.

Because it was a very special thing—to have your own cat in your own home.

Whenever he stayed overnight at Satoru's, sleeping on the futon beside his bed, he'd often be woken in the early hours by four feet clomping over him. Feeling the weight of a cat's paws pressing into your shoulders in the middle of the night—not much beats that.

He would glance over and see Hachi curled up in a ball on top of Satoru's chest. Perhaps finding it too hard to breathe, Satoru, still asleep, would slide the cat beside him. Lucky guy, Kosuke thought. If he were my cat, we could sleep together and I would let him walk all over me.

"My father seems to have taken a liking to Hachi, and I'm thinking, maybe, if we find another stray kitten, he might let me keep it."

"That'd be great! Then Hachi would have a friend."

The idea made Satoru happy, and on the way to and from swimming club he'd kept an eye out for another box with a kitten inside it.

But there never was another cardboard box with a kitten inside left under the housing complex sign.

Of course, it was a good thing that no more poor cats were abandoned. Because, even if they had found another cat, Kosuke's father still wouldn't have let him keep it.

Two years had passed since Hachi had gone to live at Satoru's. Kosuke and Satoru were now in the sixth grade of elementary school.

As autumn shed its leaves, their school organized a residential trip. Three days, two nights, in Kyoto. Kosuke could do without the temples—they all looked the same to him—but he was overjoyed to be staying away overnight with his friends, far from home.

And having more spending money than he'd ever imagined to buy souvenirs with was exciting, too. There were plenty of things he wanted to buy for himself, but he also had to remember to buy presents for his family.

One day, when they were in a souvenir shop, Satoru had a worried look on his face. "What's wrong?" asked Kosuke.

"Um, I'm wondering which one to buy."

Satoru was looking at various kinds of facial blotting paper on a cosmetics display.

"Mom asked me to buy some blotting paper, but I've forgotten which brand she wanted."

"Aren't they all the same?"

Satoru didn't seem to know one way or the other, so Kosuke said, "Why don't you buy her gift another time?"

"Okay, I guess I'll get something for Dad."

"Yeah, you should. I'll get something for my dad, too."

They wandered around a few shops, and Kosuke was the first to decide what to get. A good-luck *maneki-neko* cat keyring, the cat with a banner on its back that read "Success in Business." Of course, there was an ulterior motive behind this choice: his father might begin to like cats.

"Oh—that's great!" Satoru's eyes sparkled at the comical expression on the *maneki-neko* cat's face. "But we don't have a family business, so that slogan wouldn't work."

"There're lots of others besides 'Success in Business.'"

Satoru figured that the two slogans on banners that made most sense for his father were "Health Comes First" and "Road Safety." A third read "Harmony in the Home," but he wasn't exactly sure what that meant.

Satoru ended up picking the keyring with the "Road Safety" banner, because he thought the *maneki-neko* cat resembled Hachi.

He hadn't bought the blotting paper for his mother, but said he'd look for some the following day.

But after lunch the next day, Satoru was gone. When their class assembled, their teacher explained that "Miyawaki-kun had to return home before us."

"Ah—poor Satoru!"

His classmates all murmured to each other how sorry they were. They imagined themselves in Satoru's place, having to go home early.

"Sawada-kun, do you know why?"

Kosuke had heard nothing. Satoru had gone home without saying a thing even to his best friend, so something very serious must have happened.

And Satoru hadn't even bought the blotting paper for his mother. She'll be disappointed, Kosuke thought, when only his father gets a souvenir.

That's it! Kosuke had a sudden flash of inspiration.

I'll buy it for him, that whatchamacallit blotting paper. But how am I going to work out which brand she wants?

As he was puzzling over this, their school group went on a visit to Kinkakuji, the Temple of the Golden Pavilion. This glittery temple was unique, totally different from all the sober-looking ones they'd seen up till then. There were squeals of disbelief among the students when they saw it. "Man, that's gaudy!" was the consensus. If only Satoru could be here to see it, Kosuke thought, his heart aching.

During their free time, a couple of girls in his class were hanging out in a souvenir shop, and when he spied them, Kosuke was struck by another flash of inspiration.

The girls will know! Blotting paper is something girls use.

"Hey!" Kosuke called over to the girls, who were twittering away to each other like a pair of chirping birds.

"Do you know a brand of blotting paper? It's supposed to be kind of famous?"

They both shot back the same reply.

"You mean Yojiya. Yojiya! They have it in that store over there."

The girls were about to head over there themselves, so Kosuke went with them.

The cheapest blotting paper was over three hundred yen and, thinking how much spending money he had left, Kosuke hesitated.

But Kosuke felt sorry for Satoru, having to go home in the middle of the school trip. And he was Satoru's best friend.

Satoru probably feels worse about not getting the gift for his mother than having to go home early, he thought. And Kosuke was the only one who understood that.

He had no clue what was so special about this blotting paper, but he went ahead and bought a pack, with its distinctive drawing of a *kokeshi* doll on the wrapping. The package was so thin and flimsy-looking he was doubtful that Satoru's mother would really want it, but that's what Satoru had decided on.

"Sawada-kun, did your mother ask you to buy Yojiya paper?"

"Nope. Satoru's mother asked him, and he was searching for it in all the shops. But he went back without buying any..."

"You are such a good guy, Sawada-kun!" the girls gushed. It was not a bad feeling.

"Miyawaki-kun's mom will love it. It's a famous brand."

Is it really that famous? Kosuke was surprised, and at the same time relieved. He was convinced now that Satoru's mother would appreciate the gift, no matter how flimsy it seemed.

I should have bought the same thing for my mother, he thought, but he'd already bought her a present the day before. Buying two presents for her would push him over budget, and he could picture his father's face. He abandoned the idea.

They arrived home on the evening of the third day.

"I'm back!"

Kosuke held out the presents he'd bought and was about to tell his parents all about the trip when his father poked him.

"Stop messing around!"

But all he was doing was giving them their presents. The thought made him want to cry.

His mother had a serious look in her eyes. "Change your clothes, we're going over to Satoru's."

"Satoru had to leave early. Has something happened?"

His mother looked down, searching for how to put it, but his father didn't mince his words.

"Satoru's parents passed away."

Passed away. The words didn't register, and Kosuke stood there blankly.

"They died!" his father grunted.

The moment Kosuke understood, the tears started to flow. It was as if a dam had broken.

"Stop your blubbering," his father said, poking him again, but the tears wouldn't stop.

Satoru—*Satoru, Satoru* ... My god ...

Kosuke had gone over to Satoru's just the day before they had left for their school trip. He had been playing with Hachi and Satoru's mother had said, "You have to get up early tomorrow for your school trip, so you'd better be getting home soon. You're welcome to play with Hachi anytime." Kosuke suddenly fell silent.

"It was a car accident. They swerved to avoid a bicycle that came out of nowhere ..."

They missed the bike, but the two of them didn't make it.

"Today's the wake, so we should go."

Kosuke changed into the clothes his mother had laid out for him and the three of them set off. Just as they reached the bottom of the slope leading to the housing complex, Kosuke realized he'd forgotten something.

"You can get it later!"

He stood up to his father, telling them they could go on ahead, and finally managed to persuade him to give him the house key.

"What an idiot!" he heard his father mutter as he trotted on.

The wake was being held at the local community center. A couple of women dressed in black scurried around, and Satoru sat vacantly in front of the two coffins at the altar.

"Satoru!" Kosuke called out.

"Um," Satoru said, nodding. It was as if his mind was else-where. Kosuke had no idea what to say.

"Here you go."

Kosuke pulled out a thin paper packet from his pocket. The present he'd run back to fetch when his father had called him an idiot.

"The blotting paper your mother wanted. It's Yojiya."

Satoru burst into tears; he dropped his head while his small body shook with his sobbing. It was only later, when Kosuke had grown up, that he understood the full meaning of the word "lament."

A young woman came over quickly and huddled over him. She spoke in Satoru's ear, and from the way she was rubbing his back to comfort him, she seemed to know him well.

"Are you a friend of Satoru's?" she asked.

"Yes, I am," Kosuke replied, standing up straight.

"Would you take him home so he can have a rest? This is the first time he's cried since he got back."

Kosuke said he would.

The woman's eyes, puffy from crying herself, broke into a smile.

"Thank you," she said.

Throughout the funeral, Satoru had sat rigidly next to the young woman. There were other people there who were ap-parently relatives, but they didn't seem so close to him.

Satoru's classmates had gone, too, to light incense and

pray. All the girls sobbed, but Satoru had greeted them without shedding any tears himself.

Kosuke was impressed by how Satoru had held up. But, at the same time, it felt as if his friend had drifted away somehow and wasn't really there. If Kosuke were in Satoru's place, if his father—the one who had called him an idiot—and his mother had passed away at the same time, he knew he wouldn't be able to hold it together like that.

Kosuke took Satoru by the hand and led him home. On the way, Satoru's words were broken up by tears.

"The good-luck charm for my father came too late. And I didn't get a present for Mom ... Thank you for buying it ..."

Only Kosuke could have worked out what he was saying, so incoherent with sobs were his words.

When they got to Satoru's house, Hachi was waiting on that day's newspaper near the front door. He seemed unfazed by Satoru crying like an animal and padded toward the living room as if guiding them. When Satoru collapsed on the sofa, Hachi jumped up on his lap and licked Satoru's hand over and over.

When they'd found Hachi he'd been only a kitten, but now he seemed more grown up than Satoru.

After the funeral, Satoru didn't come back to school. Every day, Kosuke would take homework over to his house, and they would play silently with Hachi for a while, then Kosuke would go home.

The young woman stayed at Satoru's house the entire time. It turned out she was Satoru's aunt—his mother's younger sister.

Is he going to live with her here? Kosuke wondered; he would drop in on Satoru even on days when there was no homework to deliver. His aunt knew his name, greeting him with a "Hello, Kosuke," whenever he came by. But she was quieter than Satoru's gregarious mother and the house now felt strange to him.

"I'm going to move," Satoru said one day.

The aunt was going to be Satoru's guardian, but she lived a long way away.

Ever since Satoru hadn't come back to school, Kosuke had had an inkling that this might happen, but when it did it felt as if a hole had opened up in his heart.

He knew that whining about it wasn't going to change anything. He stroked Hachi as he lay curled up on Satoru's lap, without saying a word. Today, too, Hachi was gently licking Satoru's hand.

"But Hachi will go with you, won't he?"

That way, Satoru wouldn't be so lonely.

But Satoru shook his head.

"I can't take Hachi with me. My aunt moves around a lot with work."

And Satoru, too, looked like he knew that whining about it wasn't going to change anything. But that's just too much to bear, Kosuke thought.

"What'll happen to him?"

"Some other relatives say they'll take him."

"Do you know them well?"

Satoru shook his head. This made Kosuke angry. How could Hachi be taken in by people Satoru didn't even know?

"I'll ... I'll ask if we can have Hachi at our place!"

Hachi had been looked after by Kosuke half the time anyway. If Kosuke could take care of Hachi, then Satoru could come to his place to see him.

Even his father had shown an interest in Hachi whenever he visited.

But his father's view hadn't changed a bit. "No way! A cat? Are you kidding?"

"But Satoru's mom and dad are dead! And now, if Hachi has to stay with people he doesn't even know, think how sad he'll feel!"

"He knows them. They're relatives."

"Satoru said he doesn't know them!"

Distant relatives you hardly ever see are, to a child, like total strangers. Friends are much closer. Why don't adults understand that?

"In any case, it wouldn't work. Cats live ten, twenty years sometimes! Do you want to take responsibility for it your entire life?"

"Yes!"

"That's pretty cheeky for someone who's never earned a penny in his life."

His mother, perhaps thinking this was getting out of hand, stepped in on Kosuke's side, but his father still wouldn't budge.

"I feel sorry for Satoru," his father went on, "but these are two different things. Go and tell him you can't do it!"

There was no way a sixth-grade boy was going to make him change his mind, so Kosuke headed toward Satoru's, crying fat tears all the way. His legs felt like lead as he climbed up the slope from the bottom of the housing complex.

When they had first found Hachi, Satoru had done everything he possibly could to enable Kosuke to have him. His attempts had been misguided, but he had given it his all, done his very best.

And the upshot was that Hachi had gone to live in Satoru's house.

"I'm so sorry," Kosuke said, still crying, his head on his chest. "My dad said I can't have him."

Damn you, Dad. Don't you see what Satoru means to your son?

"It's okay," Satoru said, smiling through his own tears. "Thank you for asking."

On the day Satoru moved, Kosuke was there to see him off. Unbelievably, Kosuke's father came with him. "Of course I'm coming," his father had said, "since we know Satoru so well."

Seeing his best friend off before he moved away, Kosuke had never felt such deep contempt for his father.

At first, the boys exchanged letters and phone calls frequently, but as the days passed, the calls and letters naturally became less regular. One reason for this was Kosuke's shame at having shirked his duty toward his friend by not taking Hachi in.

If they had been able to see each other from time to time, their closeness would have eased his sense of awkwardness, but as they were not able to meet, time only made his feelings of guilt grow.

However, they never stopped sending each other New Year cards.

These always included a brief note saying that they should get together sometime, and they continued through high school and on into college. But the intervening years in which they hadn't seen each other made it all the harder to arrange to meet again.

At the Adult's Day ceremony, all Kosuke's old classmates were reunited to celebrate their turning twenty. Many who now lived outside the prefecture came back especially. But Satoru wasn't among them. Where was he attending his Adult's Day ceremony? Kosuke wondered.

Kosuke and his classmates must have had fun at the ceremony, because afterward, for a while at least, they continued to get together on various occasions. It was still a bit soon for a high-school reunion, but it was just the right time to wax nostalgic about elementary- and junior-high-school days.

Kosuke, who still lived in the prefecture, was put in charge of organizing the elementary-school reunion. It was decided that all his sixth-grade classmates should be invited.

As he was in charge, he decided to send an invitation to Satoru.

Satoru phoned in reply. His voice had not changed. Though they hadn't talked in years, their conversation was as lively as if no time at all had passed. Satoru rattled on and on, as if making up for all the years of silence.

"It was fun talking to you again. Well, see you!" Satoru said, and hung up. Moments later, he called again. He'd forgotten to mention the class reunion. Of course he would come.

After this, they kept in touch more regularly. Satoru was living in Tokyo, but now that they were adults, distance wasn't so much of an obstacle.

Satoru graduated from a college in Tokyo and got a job in the city. Kosuke graduated from a nearby college and found a job locally.

It was three years ago now that Kosuke had taken over his father's photographic studio.

Even after Kosuke had grown up, he and his father didn't get on, and when his father's health failed he shut up shop and moved to the countryside a short distance away. He was from a family of local landowners, so he had various plots of land in the area.

For a time, his father kept the photo studio closed. But after a while, keeping it at all seemed like too much trouble so he decided to sell it off. He'd often announced his intention to do this, but even so it made Kosuke a bit sad.

He'd been around photos ever since he was a child. His father, hot-tempered and overbearing most of the time, became cheerful and kind when teaching him about photography, and once he'd even given him an old camera. Kosuke had picked up a lot about photography, or at least his father's version of it, and when he was older he had helped out occasionally with photo sessions at the studio.

It was only through photography that he and his father had got along. Which meant that now that their connection with photography had ended, their relationship could only get worse.

And Kosuke couldn't bear that. He talked things over with his wife, and urged on, too, by the fact that his own job wasn't going well, he told his father not to sell off the studio but to let him take it over.

His father was unexpectedly overjoyed, and nearly burst into tears.

Ah, even this late in the game, maybe this would mark a change for the better.

"At least that's what I thought . . ." Kosuke almost spat the words out.

"Did you two have a bad argument or something?" Satoru asked anxiously.

"What with my father being so arrogant and selfish, maybe I shouldn't have tried so hard to be a good son."

After he had reopened the photo studio, his father still interfered, turning up and meddling.

He'd give his opinions on how to run the place, what direction the business should go in, and generally boss Kosuke around. On top of this, he'd make inappropriate remarks to Kosuke's wife.

"You'd better have a child soon so there'll be someone to take over the studio," he told her.

Kosuke and his wife were having trouble conceiving, and this was causing them a lot of stress. Kosuke's mother would sometimes warn her husband to watch his tongue, but hearing candid advice from his wife only made him more obstinate, a condition he never seemed to outgrow.

Finally, Kosuke's wife conceived a child. That had been last year. But during the first trimester of the pregnancy, when things were touch and go, she had a miscarriage.

His wife was deeply upset, and she found the words his father spoke in an attempt to comfort her extremely hurtful.

"Well," he had said, "at least we know now you can have children."

Kosuke was incensed. *Why is this man my father? I don't know how many times since I was a child I have felt this way about him. Ever since the day he rejected Hachi.*

"After that, my wife went back to her parents' place. Her parents, naturally, were furious. Even if I try to apologize, they don't want to listen."

His father showed no remorse at all. "Young women these days are so touchy," was all he could say.

"Sometimes I just wish he'd drop down dead." Kosuke blurted this out as if to himself, and quickly apologized. "Sorry about that," he added. Perhaps he'd inherited this insensitivity from his father. The idea appalled him.

"Don't worry about it," Satoru said, smiling. "There are all kinds of parent–child relationships. I never wanted my parents to die. But if I'd had other parents, I don't know how I would have felt. If your father had been my father, Kosuke, I don't know if I would have been able to love him." He burst out laughing. "Some people really shouldn't become parents. There's no absolute guarantee when it comes to the love between a parent and their child."

This was an unexpected view, coming from Satoru.

"I hope your wife will come back soon," he added.

"I don't know. It's not just her father-in-law she's upset with."

She must be disgusted with her husband, who had never been able to stand up to his father. Kosuke had a habit of swallowing whatever he wanted to say. Repeated patterns of childhood behavior have long-term consequences. All Kosuke ever did was mumble ineffectually about the ridiculous things his father said in that high-handed tone of his.

"Does your father still really meddle that much?"

"And we don't have as many customers these days, either."

People weren't going to photographic studios on special occasions like they used to. It was all part of the changing times, but Kosuke's father blamed it on his son; he thought he was spineless. And he started interfering even more, saying he needed to take charge of the business again. And still, Kosuke could never bring himself to stand up to his father and argue back.

∾

M e, on the other hand, I'm not like that. If things aren't good, I have no problem saying so. Because cats are creatures that can say no.

And the idea of being taken into the home of a man because he hoped that his wife, who likes cats, would be tempted back? I swear, with all the feline dignity I can muster, this gets a definite no from me.

"I wonder if Nana's finally got used to it here."

Kosuke stood up from the sofa and knelt beside my basket, placing his hand gently on the top.

Just try it—try pulling me out by force from this basket and I swear I'll scratch so many lines on your face you'll be able to play checkers on it for the next three months.

Chi chi chi—Kosuke made friendly little sounds and stuck his hand into the basket. I hissed and bared my teeth. Yep, that's off limits. Cross that line and, believe me, you'll live to regret it.

"He still doesn't seem to want to come out."

Kosuke withdrew his hand.

"Hmm. Doesn't look like it's going to work."

"You know …" Satoru began hesitantly. "If you're going to get a cat, I think it might be better if you and your wife find a new one together."

"What do you mean?"

"If you take my cat, it'll be like you're getting back at your father for Hachi."

"I'm sure he doesn't even remember rejecting Hachi."

"But you do."

At this, Kosuke fell silent.

I'm not denying that Kosuke wanted to take me for the sake of their friendship. But I wouldn't let him deny, either, that taking me, with my resemblance to Hachi, would have *something* to do with ghosts of the past.

Neither would I let him maintain that it had nothing to do with his wife having left him because of that difficult father of his.

"I think it would be good if you and your wife got a brand-new cat," Satoru said. "One with no strings attached."

Kosuke pouted like a child. "I loved Hachi. I really wanted to adopt him back then."

"They look similar, but Nana is his own cat. He's not Hachi."

"But you felt it was fate when you met Nana, because he looks like Hachi, didn't you? If you were fated to have Nana, then it should be my fate, too."

Jeez. *Humans*. Even when they grow up, they just don't get things. Makes me sick.

"My Hachi died. Back when I was in high school. Your Hachi, Kosuke, is still alive."

That's right. Satoru, in his mind, had already laid Hachi to rest and moved on. So Hachi's place and my place were different.

But that's not true of you, is it, Kosuke? You know in your head that Hachi's dead, but emotionally you can't accept it, right?

If you don't mourn a dead cat properly, you'll never get over it. Even if you feel able to mourn the death of a cat you've heard nothing about for years, it's a little late to feel truly sad about it, isn't it? One other thing:

You want me to replace Hachi, Kosuke. Up until now, Satoru has loved me as Nana, but now you expect me to be Hachi's stand-in? *Not going to happen!*

And even worse is your troublesome father and wounded wife being added to the mix. I am an exceptionally wise cat, but there's no way I'm going to be part of that drama, burdened with all those depressing human relationships as they fondle me. It's more than I want to take on.

"You and your wife should find a new cat and make him

your own. Leave your father out of it. He might complain, but just ignore him and get a cat, if that's what you want to do."

Kosuke didn't reply, but he looked like he finally understood.

So when he stuck his hand inside the basket again I allowed him to stroke me, as a kind of farewell gift.

It's about time you cut the strings and got over your father. Cats, you know, are independent from their parents six months after they're born.

Satoru put me and my basket back into the silver van. He stood on the pavement, talking with Kosuke. He seemed reluctant to say good-bye.

"Oh, by the way," Satoru said, slapping his forehead as if remembering something. "In the city, they have photographic studios that take photos of pets, and they're really popular. There are more people than you'd think who want to have cute photos of their pets."

Kosuke seemed quite keen on the idea. "Have you had professional photos taken of Nana?"

Satoru smiled mischievously. "Not yet. But if the Sawada Studio becomes a pet studio, then maybe I will."

Kosuke broke into a smile. "It'd be fun to hurl a new business idea in my father's face, too."

Satoru was now in the van. He wound down the window.

"One more thing," he said to Kosuke. "When I was twenty, you invited me to a class reunion, remember?"

"Oh, that old story." Kosuke laughed.

"It made me so happy."

"Why are you bringing that up now?"

"'Cause I don't think I ever told you how happy it made me."

"Oh, *stop*," Kosuke said, trying to change the subject.

"I won't," Satoru said jokily. "Thank you. I never thought I'd get a chance to come back to this town."

Satoru finally drove off.

"Sorry, Nana," Satoru said, turning toward me in the backseat. "I thought it was better for him to get his own cat than to take you. But I'll find someone to have you, someone I can trust completely."

No worries. I mean, I didn't ask you to do this in the first place.

If you had forced me to stay there, things would have been pretty terrible for you and Kosuke, you know? By that, I mean half a year's worth, perhaps, of checkerboards on your faces.

Satoru glanced at me in the backseat, where I was now sitting in a tidy ball, my tail around my front legs. He let out a yelp.

"Nana! How did you get out?"

Didn't you know? That lock on the basket doesn't work very well, and it's easy-peasy to unlock it from the inside.

"So you can open it? I had no idea. I'll have to buy a new one."

You find out I can open the basket, and that's all you can say? Even that day when you took me to the one place I never, ever want to go, the vet's, I didn't try to run away.

"On second thought, maybe there's no need. Even if you've known how to get out all along, you still listened to me."

Exactly. Satoru should be thankful I'm such an exceptionally bright cat.

I stretched up, placing my front paws on the passenger window, and enjoyed the passing scenery for a while, then curled up on the seat.

Some kind of rock music was playing on the car radio, and the bass sounds vibrated in my stomach. Not exactly my thing.

Cats have their own preferences when it comes to music. Did you know that?

I pressed my ears down and waved my tail around in an attempt to make my feelings known to Satoru. It didn't take him long to understand.

"Oh, I see, you don't like this. What's on the stereo, I wonder?"

Satoru switched to the car stereo and a light orchestral melody started playing. Okay, this wasn't so bad.

"My mother used to like this. Paul Mauriat."

Hm, not bad at all. I could picture doves about to fly off, a happy vision from the feline perspective.

"I never knew you liked cars so much, Nana. If I'd known, I would have taken you to all kinds of places."

Saying I like cars is a little inaccurate. Aren't you sort of forgetting that a car broke my leg?

I just like this silver van, that's all. 'Cause it was mine even before I met Satoru.

Okay, so whose place are you going to take me to next?

~

After Kosuke had waved off Satoru and Nana, he went back inside and found a text on his phone.

It was from his wife.

Did you take the cat?

He was about to reply, but decided to call instead.

He had a feeling that this time she might answer.

The phone rang seven times. Nana's lucky seven.

"Hello?" His wife's tone was flat and a little distant.

Now it was up to Kosuke to cheerfully, delicately, soften that hard voice.

"I was thinking," he said evenly. "What about if the two of us got our own new cat?"

2

The Unsentimental Farmer

The day we set off again, music filled the silver van once more, the kind that sounds like a magician is about to whisk a dove from a hat.

Satoru said the title was "Necklace of Olive." How come there was no dove in the title? If it were up to me, I'd put one in. How about calling it "The Special Relationship Between a Dove and a Silk Hat"?

"It's nice to have good weather again today, isn't it, Nana?"

Satoru was in a great mood. All cats get sleepy when it rains, and I was wondering: does weather affect humans physically, too?

"Going for a drive isn't much fun if it's not sunny."

Ah, so it was a question of mood. Humans are so easygoing. A cat's behavior is controlled by real-life factors, and for strays the weather can be a matter of life and death. Our success rate in hunting changes, too.

"We'll take a break at the next service station."

Unlike when we went to Kosuke's place, the road we were taking on that day had very few places to stop. Satoru said it was called a motorway. Basically the only time the silver van stopped was when Satoru announced that we were heading to a *service station.*

Satoru said this was the road we had to take if we intended to travel far away, and this trip was indeed a long one. It was the previous morning that the silver van had left home. We drove along the highway all day, then stayed overnight at a place where they allow pets.

With it being such a long trip, the space in the van had been compartmentalized. So, if you'll excuse me a second.

As I slipped off the passenger seat toward the back of the van, Satoru asked, "Something wrong?" and glanced at me.

"Ah, sorry . . ."

Yeah. My toilet was on the floor at the back. A new one Satoru had bought, which had a hood so the litter didn't fly all over the place.

This way, Satoru and I could go as far as we wanted in our silver van.

I thought it would be great if we could travel together like this for the rest of our lives.

"Nana, we're just going to pull into a service station—"

Okey-dokey, I answered vaguely, raking up the litter between my legs.

Once Satoru had parked at the service station, he pulled out my food and water bowls from the back. He placed them on the floor of the van side by side, filling one bowl with crunchies and the other with water from a plastic bottle.

"I'm going to go to the toilet, too."

Satoru hurriedly shut the door and strolled off. He looked like he really had to go, but he was such a good owner he had taken care of my needs first.

I was wetting my whistle with the water when I heard a tapping on the window. Not *again*.

I glanced behind me and then up to see a young couple, faces plastered against the glass, staring in my direction. The pair had goofy smiles.

"A cat!"

You got that right. A cat I am. So? A cat eating his crunchies isn't so rare a sight, is it?

"Oh, look—it's eating. How sweet!"

"So sweet!"

Hey, you idiotic couple. How would you like it if somebody pointed at you while you were eating? And today happens to be a chicken-breast-and-gourmet-seafood blend.

How come cat lovers spot me every time? Whenever we take a break, they swarm around me. Pretty amazing, if you think about it.

If you guys were the ones who fed me, then I'd be as sweet to you as the quality of the food merited, but Satoru's the one who feeds me. So let me focus on my food. Okay?

I decided to ignore them and dived back into my crunchies.

With some screeches and giggles, they seemed to give up and wander away.

But only moments later I felt someone's red-hot gaze on me. I looked up despite myself, and this time it was a scary-looking, goblin-like old man's face plastered to the window.

Yikes! I jerked away on reflex, and the old man looked really hurt. Come on—anybody would shudder if they were suddenly confronted by that kind of face while they were having a snack. Not my fault, now, is it?

The old man looked upset but kept his face up against the window, staring at me.

"I'm guessing you like cats?"

This from Satoru, who'd come back. The old man, a bit flustered, replied, "Sure is a cute little kitty." *Cute little kitty?*

I looked up and meowed. On the other side of the window, Satoru smiled and nodded.

"Would you like to stroke him?"

"Are you sure?"

The old man started to blush like a girl. Satoru opened the door and I clambered over to the seat. The old man reached out and I let him stroke me. His face began to glow. But just then—

"No way! A cat!"

The shriek came from a clump of *gyaru*—girls with dyed-blonde hair and thick makeup—who were passing by.

"I want to stroke it! Can we touch him after you?"

Get lost! I bared my teeth and made my fur stand on end, and the group of *gyaru* shrieked again: "Oh my god—he's angry!" and ran off.

"But I wanted to give him a stroke—" the tall one whined.

"It's okay. That kind of cat with those eyebrow markings isn't that cute anyway."

Excuse me?! This insult was so unfounded my face went into a kind of flehmen response. I curled back my upper lip and bared my front teeth like a tiger.

"You *are* cute, Nana! Very cute!" Satoru hurriedly interjected. "Those girls are a bit loud, and I'm sure their sense of what's beautiful is different from most people's. Let's just let it go."

"No, he really is a cute cat," the old man said. "Nana, you said his name is?"

"Yeah. Because his tail's hooked into the shape of a seven."

I didn't think we needed to explain the origin of my name to every passing stranger, but Satoru was always so conscientious when it came to things like that.

"Is he maybe the type that doesn't let people touch him much?"

"Yes, he's very choosy about who he allows to touch him when we're out and about."

"I see," the old man said, smiling even more broadly. Then he gave me one final lingering pat on the middle of my back and walked off.

"Kind of unusual, isn't it, Nana, for you to let a passerby stroke you for so long?"

True enough. How should I put it? I was making amends— a sort of atonement. No need to analyze it any further.

The van had been driving along for a while when I next stretched up to look out of the passenger window. The sea!

"I think you'll like the sea, Nana."

Until then, I'd only seen it on the TV in Satoru's front room, which I used to watch from my blanket in the corner. To see it now for real was going to be amazing.

And it was! The sparkling, deep-green water was completely stunning, but more than that was the idea that underneath that water lurked all the delicacies that made up my gourmet seafood blend. Oops! I had started to drool at the thought of it.

"If, like last time, you end up coming back with me, let's stop by the sea properly."

What? Stop by the sea? Might I be lucky enough to catch one or two of those delicacies?

The sea was soon out of sight, and I drifted off for a bit. When I lazily opened my eyes again the scenery had become tranquil and countrified. Now we were sliding past green rice paddies and broad fields like a whirligig.

"Oh, you're up? We're almost there."

Just as Satoru said, the van soon pulled up in the front yard of a farmhouse. It seemed functionally constructed, large and practical. Nearby was an annex of sorts, and a shed. Beside it was parked a smallish truck.

I took the initiative and leaped onto the backseat, into the opened basket. I've learned that when you go into an unknown house, it's best and safest to be in a place you're used to, one where you can barricade yourself in.

Satoru opened the back door and picked up the basket with me inside.

"Satoru Miyawaki!"

At the sound of a welcoming voice, I peered through the bars and saw a man in work clothes and a straw hat heading toward Satoru, hand held high.

"Yoshimine, how have you been?" Satoru's voice was excited, too. "You're looking good."

"I work outdoors all the time, so your body naturally gets strong. Haven't you become a little thinner?"

"Have I? Guess it's the unhealthy city lifestyle."

The two of them clapped each other on the back and headed toward the main house.

"Did you have any trouble finding my place?"

"No, the sat-nav made it easy."

"Still, I didn't think you'd come all this way from Tokyo by car. Flying would have been faster, and cheaper. Going by road must have been a bit pricey?"

Absolutely. You have the tolls on the motorway, service stations, the pet-friendly little hotel we stayed in last night. By the time we got here, Satoru had opened his wallet several times.

"But if I had flown, then Nana would have been stored in the luggage hold, which is dark and noisy. One time, I took another cat on a plane and it was terrified for the entire day after we landed. Cats can't understand why they're in a situation like that, and I'd feel bad if Nana had to go through it."

Okay, I might be terrified, but I'm a little offended that he'd think that Hachi could make it, but I couldn't. Surely I'm more intrepid than Hachi. After all, until I was an adult, I survived as a stray on the streets.

Instead of worrying about me, you should worry about all the money you've spent on this trip.

Inside the main house, Yoshimine showed us into the living room. Satoru placed my basket in a corner and opened the door.

Yoshimine was crouching in front of my basket.

"Mind if I take a look at Nana?" he said, peering in.

"Sure, but it might take a bit of time for him to feel comfortable enough to come out."

"No problem."

What do you mean, *no problem*? I tilted my head in puzzlement and, just at that instant, a thick arm shot into the cage.

Hey, what—?

The fat arm grabbed me by the scruff of the neck and,

without so much as a by-your-leave, dragged me out, then dangled me high up in the air.

Wh-wha-what the hell do you think you're doing, you barbarian!

"Good! He's a proper cat."

What the hell do you mean by *that*?

"Hey!"

Satoru, horrified, gave Yoshimine a healthy shove in the back. "What do you think you're doing?"

"I just wanted to make sure he's a real cat," Yoshimine explained, holding me against him with his thick arm. I tried to kick myself free, but that thick arm just took my kicks and didn't budge an inch.

"What do you mean?"

"Look, you hold him like this, see?"

"Don't hold him like that!"

"If his back legs fold up when you do this, it means he's a real cat."

Let me go! I put my legs together and kicked off against Yoshimine's arm, flopping around like a salmon. Finally, I was able to break free.

I twisted my body around and landed perfectly on my four paws. Keeping my belly low to the ground, I turned to meet Yoshimine's eye, and he said, "Whoa!" and clapped his hands.

"One fine cat you've got here. Well coordinated, and smart, too. An outstanding cat. I underestimated him."

"Yeah, I guess so."

That can't be true. Of course I'm well bred, *but still*. Satoru interrupted, in sync with me: "But still—that's not the point!" Great minds think alike. "Why did you grab Nana by the neck like that? It startled him!"

"The reason is, I found a stray recently that isn't a real cat. If Nana turned out to be like that one, there wouldn't be much point, from a farmer's perspective, in having him. So I just wanted to check him out."

This unpleasant guy came over to try to play with my tail, which I was waving slowly to show my displeasure.

I spun around, only to find an orange tabby male kitten beside me. He'd appeared out of nowhere and was meowing and trying to cling to my hooked tail. What a pain.

Yoshimine grabbed the kitten by the scruff of the neck and picked him up. The kitten's legs drooped down in a line.

"This one isn't a real cat. See?"

True, this kitten didn't seem equipped with the natural abilities of most cats. He was the kind—like Hachi—that would never catch a mouse. Even if he could hone his skills through training, he would never be a true hunter like me.

"He's still just a kitten, you shouldn't treat him so roughly ..."

Satoru reached his hand out, fluttering it in the air in a *stop that* gesture. Yoshimine thrust the kitten at him.

"Here. Feel free to stroke him, if you like."

"I'd love to."

Satoru was a dyed-in-the-wool cat lover, like I said. Go ahead and get all lovey-dovey with that kitten. See if I care.

∽

It had been a long time since Yoshimine had received an e-mail from his former junior-high classmate Satoru Miyawaki.

He had just been thinking about him when the e-mail arrived.

After a few quick words to bring him up to date, Satoru issued his request.

I know this is a bit sudden, but could you take my cat for me?

He's really precious to me, he went on, *but unavoidable circumstances make it impossible for me to keep him, and I'm looking for someone to adopt him.*

There were two things Yoshimine could read in this message.

One was that his cat-devoted friend had once more found a cat he loved, and two, that once again he was having to part ways with it.

When it came to cats, Daigo Yoshimine could take them or leave them. If there was one in the house, he'd notice it and look after it, but he wasn't passionate enough about them to adopt one himself. He felt the same way about dogs and birds.

But having a cat on a farm did have its advantages. On

farms, mice inevitably caused damage, and a cat was a pretty good means of control.

He tapped out a reply.

I don't think I'd look after a cat the way you do—I treat them like cats, not like pets—but if you're okay with that, I'd be happy to take him off your hands. If you can't find anyone else, then let me know. Rest assured, I'll make sure he's looked after.

Satoru wrote back thanking him. *I've promised to show him to one other person first,* he said, *but if that doesn't work out, I'll be counting on you.*

A month later, Satoru wrote back again, asking if he could bring the cat over for Yoshimine to meet.

And, by coincidence, it was during this time that Yoshimine happened to find the kitten.

"I was driving down the highway in my truck when I saw him lying by the side of the road like a limp dishrag. I wouldn't have been able to forgive myself if I had just left him there."

"I see …"

Satoru seemed to melt with the orange tabby kitten on his lap. Cat lovers have a special place in their hearts for kittens.

"You did a good job bringing up this teeny guy. Was it hard?"

"I needed the vet a few times. But there're other folk in the neighborhood who have cats, and plenty of people ready to give advice."

Because it was the countryside, people weren't all that particular about the way they brought cats up.

"It was a lot easier once he started eating cat food."

Satoru burst out laughing. "I'm trying to imagine you feeding a kitten milk from a bottle. You're lucky, aren't you," Satoru said to the kitten, tickling him vigorously under the chin, "to be taken in by such a kind owner?"

"I'm not that kind. I was hoping he'd catch a mouse or two around the place, but he's not a real cat and I feel a bit let down."

"So, now that he's recovered, are you going to throw him out of the house?"

Yoshimine looked put out by Satoru's teasing tone.

Satoru stroked the kitten in his lap in contented silence. Then he said, "I get it now. That's why you were asking whether Nana was a real cat or not."

"If I bring up two of them and they're both useless, then all that cat food is a total waste."

"I knew you wouldn't turn Nana down."

"Well, I can't exactly refuse a guest who's driven all the way here from Tokyo just for a cat."

"I get it," Satoru responded, as if he didn't really accept this explanation.

"By the way, what's the kitten's name?"

"Chatran."

"That's pretty silly."

"Is it?"

Yoshimine had asked around the neighbors who owned cats, and one person had said, "An orange tabby? That reminds me of Chatran." He liked the name and decided to use it.

"Since that movie *The Adventures of Chatran* came out, it's become a bit of a cliché to call an orange tabby Chatran."

"Hmm. I didn't know that."

And this Chatran with the silly name recognized a real cat lover and was fully relaxing in Satoru's lap, stretching his paw onto Satoru's cheek.

"This brings back memories. I used to have a cat who did this."

Satoru never named this cat he used to have to Yoshimine. He felt that if he spoke its name aloud, all the pent-up affection and sadness would break his heart again.

And even someone who knows nothing about the universal benefit of cats could understand that.

◦⌐

Yoshimine had transferred into the junior high school in the spring of his second year.

"This is Daigo Yoshimine, who will be joining us as your new classmate."

The form teacher was a striking woman who'd won some

Miss Something-or-other contest back in college, but Yoshimine had disliked her from the start.

When she explained to the class, in great detail, why he had moved to their school, she made it sound very close and intimate and oozed sympathy.

He had gritted his teeth and let her words wash over him, but what he couldn't fend off was the timing.

"Yoshimine-kun's parents are busy with their jobs, so he's transferred here and will be staying with his grandmother. We should all admire him, for enduring the loneliness of being away from his parents. I'd like you all to be friends with him."

He understood then that her overly intimate manner was because she felt sorry for him. And, deep down, that disgusted him.

Even to an immature class of junior-high-school students with little worldly experience, it was crystal clear that this was the worst possible way to introduce a new student to his classmates.

"Yoshimine-kun, why don't you say a few words?"

Yoshimine turned to face the teacher. "Why did you tell everyone about my family like that without my permission? I never asked you to."

A murmur rippled through the classroom. The teacher was taken aback, her smile faltering. "I—I thought it would help you settle in."

"No, in fact it makes me uncomfortable. I want people to be friends with me without my family being a part of it."

"I understand, but the thing is ..." the teacher mumbled. There was no way this was going to turn out well.

Yoshimine turned to face the other students.

"Hi. I'm Daigo Yoshimine. There's nothing special about my family, so I hope we can just get along like anybody else."

A deathly hush descended on the classroom. Right from the start, he'd put them off.

As for his form teacher, she looked on the verge of tears.

"Where do you want me to sit?"

Just then the bell went, signaling the end of form time, and the teacher left the classroom in a hurry.

"Just sit down on any empty chair."

It was Satoru who said this, pointing to some seats at the back.

First period was over, and while his other classmates eyed the new boy warily, keeping their distance, Satoru approached him without hesitation.

The next class was science. Yoshimine gathered his textbooks and left the classroom, with Satoru leading the way.

"Listen." Something was bothering Yoshimine, and he had to ask. "Are you being nice to me just because of what the teacher said?"

"Not at all," Satoru replied. "I thought it was all pretty childish. On both parts."

"You mean me, too?"

"That teacher likes to be super-kind to kids who have issues going on at home. She doesn't mean any harm by it."

Something about the way he said this—the desire to be kind and mean no harm—made Yoshimine feel he had something in common with Satoru, a kind of connection.

"Right after I entered this school, in freshman year, she did the same thing to me, so I get where you're coming from. When I was in elementary school, my parents died in a car accident and now I live with my aunt. But that doesn't mean I want to go out of my way to tell everybody in class about it."

The circumstances Satoru had so casually mentioned were so much more serious than Yoshimine's. So surely the teacher must have put on an even more annoying display of concern.

"But you don't need to complain about every little thing. Just take it as it comes, be grown-up about it."

A little too philosophical, aren't you, for a second-year junior high schooler? Yoshimine thought, but what Satoru said made sense, so he didn't argue.

"Still," Satoru said with a grin. "To tell you the truth, I felt good when you said that. Back when I started school, I wanted to say what you actually did say."

Yoshimine changed the subject.

"What's your name?"

"Satoru Miyawaki. Nice to meet you."

He didn't have to say anything like *Let's hang out*, for by this time they were already friends.

From day one, Yoshimine hadn't got on with his classmates or his form teacher, but being friends with Satoru made life at school go more smoothly.

Satoru had also apparently straightened things out with the teacher. Yoshimine had no idea how he had won her over, but one day she stopped him in the corridor and tearfully apologized.

"I'm so sorry, Yoshimine-kun. I didn't understand how badly you were feeling."

Yoshimine felt as if some huge misunderstanding was about to occur, but it was too much trouble to explain things, so, following the advice to be *grown-up* about it, he ended the encounter with a quick "It's okay."

"Don't worry, Yoshimine-kun," his teacher added. "I won't mention your family situation again."

So it seemed there was still some major misunderstanding about his family situation, which only Satoru correctly grasped.

"My parents," Yoshimine had explained to him, "both work really hard and love their jobs too much."

His father was in R&D at a top electronics company, while his mother worked in foreign investment for a multinational trading company. They were hardly ever at home, and Yoshimine often went days without seeing them.

"Since spring, they've both become even busier, and they can't seem to find any time for their family. Including me."

His parents had tried to offload responsibility for their son onto his older brother, and their preoccupation with work had quickly led to total neglect of the household.

"So they decided to send me to live with my grandmother on my father's side until things settled down."

But he didn't think it was a big deal, so he found it embarrassing when his teacher went all gushy over how sad he must be. Because there are lots of kids with much tougher backgrounds. Take Satoru, for instance.

"Hey, Yoshimine." A classmate called out to him from the corridor, putting an end to their conversation. "You interested in joining the judo club?"

"Nope."

The classmate's shoulders drooped in disappointment, though he didn't stop trying, dangling the possibility of him being a regular on the team. "So—what do you say?" he asked.

"I say no thanks," Yoshimine replied.

With his sturdy build, he was continually being invited to join the school sports teams, but Yoshimine turned them all down.

"Aren't you into school clubs?" Satoru asked.

"I don't like sports much," he replied. He certainly had an athletic physique, but he disliked games with too many rules.

"What about other kinds of clubs?"

"If there was a gardening club I might join."

His grandmother's family were farmers and he had always enjoyed digging in the soil. His grandfather had passed away a few years before, and his grandmother had only just been managing to keep the family plots going, so Yoshimine had been pitching in.

"There's a greenhouse in the corner of the school grounds. I wonder if anyone's using it."

The greenhouse had been on Yoshimine's mind ever since he had transferred to the school.

"I've never even thought about it. You interested?" Satoru asked.

"My grandmother's crops are all outdoors. I've never worked in a greenhouse."

"You really are into farming, aren't you?"

Yoshimine thought that was the end of the matter, but Satoru brought it up again later.

"I looked into the gardening club thing. They stopped a few years ago, because membership numbers fell. But if you're interested, the science teacher said he'd run it, even if it's just the two of us. And we can use the greenhouse."

Two things surprised Yoshimine. One, that Satoru had actually looked into it. And two, that he was planning to take part himself.

"You want to be in the club, too?" Yoshimine asked.

"I'd like to give it a try."

"But you're not into gardening or anything like that, are you?"

"I wouldn't say I'm not interested. I just haven't had any-thing to do with it up till now. I've never known any farmers."

"Really? Nobody? Not even, like, your grandfather or your grandmother?"

A total city boy, Yoshimine thought, but Satoru waved a dismissive hand.

"It's not that," he said. "My parents didn't have much to do with their relatives. My grandparents on my mother's side died when she was still young, and my father didn't seem to get on with his parents that well. The first time I met them was at my parents' funeral, and we didn't talk much."

Yoshimine understood now why Satoru's aunt had taken him in. If your parents died and your grandparents were in good health, it's likely that's where you'd go. Pretty unusual for a single woman to take a young boy in.

"I reckoned this might be my only chance to give it a go," Satoru said, laughing. "I've dreamed about living the country life. Like in Miyazaki's film *My Neighbor Totoro*, do you know it?"

And so the two of them revived the gardening club. Yoshi-mine's grandmother also invited Satoru over to their home to experience life on a working farm.

Satoru was a latchkey kid, since his aunt worked all day, so he began to go over to Yoshimine's home, and sometimes stayed over for the weekend.

"I hope you will be good friends," Yoshimine's grandmother said to Satoru—what grandmothers typically say when other children come to play. "I always wonder if Daigo"—she called him by his first name—"is getting on with the other children at school. I hope he isn't being bullied."

"I wouldn't worry about that. I don't think there's any chance Yoshimine would ever be bullied."

"What d'ya mean?" Yoshimine said, poking him in the ribs.

"You know exactly what I mean," Satoru said, poking him back.

His grandmother, who had been worried that Yoshimine might not make any friends in his new school, was overjoyed when he brought Satoru home. Very soon, she started calling him Satoru-chan.

"Shall I buy a video game or something you can play with Satoru-chan?"

She asked this because she was concerned that he might be getting bored, always helping out in the fields.

"I already have some," Yoshimine replied, "and so does Satoru."

Satoru genuinely enjoyed helping out in the fields—it was a kind of pastoral hobby.

"We're doing the gardening club at school together, too, and I think he really likes farm work," Yoshimine explained to his grandmother.

"Really? Then that's fine," his grandmother responded. "At any rate, you've made a good friend here. So I won't worry about you."

His grandmother didn't just say this once, but at every opportunity. As if reassuring herself.

"I guess Grandma still sees me as a little kid," Yoshimine said, a trifle embarrassed.

With Satoru being so good-natured, and her grandson's best friend to boot, Yoshimine's grandmother fussed over him, and Satoru grew very attached to her.

"You're lucky," he told Yoshimine. "I wish I had a grandmother like yours."

He'd never been close to his grandparents, and seemed to enjoy having a relationship with an elderly person.

"If you're okay with an old woman like me," Yoshimine's grandmother told him, "then consider this like your own grandmother's house."

Yoshimine never teased his friend about his obvious envy of his grandmother. He knew that Satoru tended to keep his distance from his aunt and had no other relatives he could become close to.

"Come over anytime. My grandmother likes you a lot, too."

One afternoon, during class, Yoshimine was feeling uncomfortably hot. He glanced out of the window and saw heat shimmering up from the ground. It was the time of year when the temperature was often over eighty-five degrees.

He suddenly pushed his chair back and stood up, causing a stir of excitement in the class.

"Yoshimine! What do you think you're doing?" his teacher scolded.

"Nothing," Yoshimine said casually, and walked out of the classroom.

"Hey!"

At times like these, it was Satoru's role to step in.

"What do you mean, nothing?" he called.

"I'll be right back."

It was Satoru, not their teacher, who ran out of the classroom after him.

"What's wrong?" he asked Yoshimine, when he finally caught up with him.

"The greenhouse. I forgot to open the vent this morning. It's so hot now, the plants are going to boil."

Inside the greenhouse, they were growing tomatoes and other vegetables, as well as tending some orchids, a hobby of the science teacher. Tomatoes don't do well in the rain so the roofed-in environment was perfect for them, but this region generally had a temperate climate and when it got too hot in the summer they suffered.

"Why not wait until break? It's only another thirty minutes."

"But it's the hottest time of the day. We have to cool it down as soon as we can."

"You could have pretended you had to go to the bathroom or something! It'll be your fault if they close down our club."

"Then you go and explain."

"Jeez," Satoru muttered, and made his way back to the classroom.

"Yoshimine's been attacked by guerrillas!"

Satoru's report had the classroom in uproar.

Though Yoshimine threw the class into chaos on such occasions, before the summer vacation they got a bumper crop of tomatoes and other vegetables and were able to save their teacher's orchids as well.

When he was sharing out the vegetables with Satoru and the teacher, Yoshimine ended up taking a portion of tomatoes that was a little larger than the others. Yoshimine's grandmother's outdoor-grown tomato plants had been hit hard by the long rainy season and hadn't yielded quite what she'd hoped.

"Take more. There are just the two of us in our house, so I don't need so many," Satoru said, and Yoshimine burst out laughing. There were only two in Yoshimine's home, too, and one of them was extremely old. Satoru had a comeback for that: "But you eat much more than I do."

In the space of one semester, Satoru had learned a lot about farming, and had picked up on the fact that Yoshimine wanted to grow greenhouse tomatoes as a sort of insurance policy against his grandmother's tomatoes failing. Grateful, Yoshimine went ahead and took three or four extra, dropping them happily into his bucket.

"I'm going back home the first week of the summer holiday," Yoshimine said.

"I get it," Satoru answered instantly. "I'll take care of the greenhouse while you're gone."

Their first crop was in already, but there were a lot more that would ripen later.

"This is the first time you've been home since you came to this school, isn't it? Hope it goes okay."

Satoru understood the situation, which is why he didn't just say, *Oh, that's nice.* Yoshimine's parents weren't taking any time off work to see their son; he was just putting in a token appearance. "If they ripen while you're away, I'll take some tomatoes over to your grandmother's."

Yoshimine's grandmother gave him a lift to the airport in her little van, and he flew back to Tokyo.

Nobody was there to meet him at Haneda airport.

He boarded the airport shuttle for the ride home, to a condo in a residential suburb. After a whole semester at his grandmother's, the apartment seemed even smaller and more cramped than before.

His parents were as preoccupied as ever.

About three days after Yoshimine had arrived home, both his parents, surprisingly, came home from work early. His mother cooked them dinner, a rare thing, and the three of them sat down together to eat.

After dinner, his mother made them tea. The whole thing had Yoshimine confused.

His father, seated opposite him at the dining table, spoke first, a serious look on his face.

"We have something important to tell you."

His mother came over and sat down next to his father. This couldn't be good.

"The thing is, Mom and I have decided to get divorced."

Ah—just as I thought, Yoshimine said to himself.

He had known that someday it would come to this.

"Daigo, do you want to come and live with me, or your mother?"

He looked at his parents' expressions and was forced to confront a reality he couldn't avoid.

His parents waited expectantly, each hoping he would choose the other.

"I'm sorry." He was finally able to squeeze out the words. "I can't decide right now. I want to think about it a little more."

His parents were clearly relieved that they wouldn't have to deal with the problem straight away.

"Can I go back to Grandma's place tomorrow?"

Confronted with the fact that neither parent wanted him, he no longer had any idea how he was supposed to behave.

Naturally, they didn't stop him, and he flew back the following day. The airline took good care of unaccompanied children, and he was actually grateful that his parents weren't there to see him off.

His grandmother came to pick him up at the airport and drove him briskly back home in her small van.

"Mom and Dad said they're getting divorced."

"Is that right?" his grandmother replied.

"I don't know which one I should live with."

"Well, it doesn't really matter, because you can live with me."

Yoshimine felt a huge lump in his throat.

"You have a good friend here, too, Daigo, so it's all okay."

You have a good friend here. It's all okay, his grandmother murmured, over and over, as if reassuring herself.

His grandmother had known what was going to happen from the moment her grandson had first come to live with her.

The lump in Yoshimine's throat grew bigger and by the time they arrived home, it had started to hurt.

"I'm going to run over to school."

He changed into his uniform. Even in the holidays, they weren't allowed at the school unless they were wearing it.

"Why don't you wait until a bit later? It's the hottest time of day now."

"I'm worried about the greenhouse."

Shaking off his grandmother's objections, Yoshimine rode his bike to the junior high. As he pumped the pedals he felt the lump in his throat sink to the pit of his stomach.

Satoru's bike was parked in the bicycle racks.

Inside the greenhouse, Yoshimine found him happily plucking tomatoes and cucumbers.

"Hey."

As Yoshimine stood in the doorway to the greenhouse, Satoru let out a funny-sounding "What the—? Weren't you supposed to come back a little later?"

"Yeah, stuff happened."

They washed the vegetables in the sink, and in the shade of the school building Yoshimine told Satoru what had happened. Out of the corner of his eye, Yoshimine watched the baseball team doing fielding practice in the shimmering heat-waves radiating from the schoolyard.

"When they left me with Grandma, I didn't think anything major was going on, since my parents had always kind of left me to my own devices. But it's turned out to be a big deal."

So the form teacher's sympathy was justified, after all.

"They were planning to get divorced all along. And they wanted me to understand that. I'm such an idiot."

Satoru had been listening in silence, but now he broke in. "That's not true," he countered. "You were just trying not to think about it."

Yoshimine felt that lump in his throat again. *Get over it*, he urged himself.

*D**aigo never gives us any trouble, and that makes things so much easier.*

If I had been a bad kid who *did* give them a hard time, *then* what would have happened?

Ever since he was little, he had known his parents were

both overly fond of their jobs and weren't particularly interested in him. Which is why he tried his best to be the kind of child who wouldn't require too much of their time and effort, the kind who wouldn't get under their feet.

Being a kid who never gave his parents any trouble would at least stop them being in a bad mood and keep things settled on the home front. In that way, Yoshimine, who was always the one holding the fort, could breathe easy.

And the few times that the whole family was together, things did go smoothly. But maybe all he'd done was to prioritize what was easy in the short term.

There's a proverb that says a child is the glue that keeps a husband and wife together. A child who was never any trouble might keep things peaceful from day to day, but when push came to shove, that child would finally come unstuck.

Maybe the kind of kid who needed more parental affection and made trouble would have been the glue that would have held their marriage together.

Enough.

Yoshimine shook his head hard to put a stop to the thoughts spinning around in it. There's no use thinking about something that can't be undone. It'll just let this lump grow bigger. It's already pretty big.

"Still," he said aloud. "Parents get divorced all the time."

He tried to say it casually, but the tail end of his words wavered.

"You had it a lot harder than me, didn't you, Satoru?"

"But I never once experienced my parents acting like I was a nuisance, because they were gone."

There was nothing Yoshimine could say to that. The lump in his throat burst at long last.

When his sobbing finally subsided, Satoru asked, "Want one?" and held out in his soiled fingers a luscious red tomato.

∽

Really, now, I thought, looking at Satoru.

I was out of the basket. Not sure why, but Satoru had left the door open, telling me to come out whenever I felt comfortable, but the thought of that tabby kitten with the stupid name, Chatran, invading my space was unbearable, truth be told.

Hey, tabby. You know your owner was abandoned by his parents, too. But the tabby was so engrossed in playing with his toy mouse he didn't hear me. When are you going to realize how pointless it is to play with a fake mouse, eh?

Having a decent conversation with an itty-bitty kitten this young was out of the question. He was of the age when he'd eat, leap around a bit, then suddenly flop down asleep in the middle of whatever he was doing, as if his batteries had run down.

Even when he was in the middle of saying something, if a breeze made the curtain flutter he would drop everything and leap at it. Was I that silly when I was his age? I think I had a bit more sense than that. Well, cats mature emotionally at different rates. I felt sorry for the poor kid, compared to a rare, wise cat such as myself.

Stitching together his fragmented history, I gathered that this orange tabby was the runt of the litter, and when his mother had moved home, he hadn't been able to keep up and got left behind.

A fact of life in the feline world. Kittens that are awkward to bring up, or slow, are easily abandoned. No matter how hard she tries, a mother cat has only so much milk, and she won't waste any on a lethargic kitten.

One of my siblings was like that. Overshadowed by the rest of us, it was the kind of kitten you were never sure was there or not, and one day we suddenly noticed it was gone, as if it had never existed.

This orange tabby was on the small side for his age; to be honest, not the type you'd expect to make it in life. Yoshimine had done a great job bringing him up. And despite him being the ill-mannered kind who'd grab you by the scruff of the neck the first time he met you, Yoshimine hadn't just looked the other way when a troublesome kitten turned up, so it was clear to me he was an individual who had a lot of love to give.

Even people who are big and strong are sometimes thrown in the gutter. If he'd been a cat, Yoshimine would have been the top priority in the litter.

Okay, be that as it may ...

You probably shouldn't have made it, little kitty, yet you've been given a new lease of life, so shouldn't you show some gratitude to Yoshimine for that? Yes, you. I'm talking to *you*.

The orange tabby looked as though he was listening for a moment, but then, clearly not getting what I was saying, he started to play around with my tail. Hmm. Guess I'll have to simplify this a bit.

Tell me, do you like Yoshimine?

I seemed to have got through. As he chewed on my tail, he nodded. Hey, that hurt. I flipped my tail up.

If you like Yoshimine, don't you want to make him happy?

The orange tabby grabbed my tail again and recommenced chomping with his mini jaws.

I told you, that hurts! I flipped it up again.

You do know Yoshimine wants cats to catch mice for him, don't you? So, if you can become a real cat who can catch mice, I'm sure Yoshimine will be very pleased.

The orange tabby stopped his chomping for a moment. I seemed to have struck a chord.

But the way you're behaving, forget it. You're useless. You couldn't even catch a lizard, let alone a mouse.

Okay, what if I teach you the basics of hunting? And not just hunting, but train you to hold your own in a fight with other cats. Yoshimine will be worried if you lose every scrap.

Putting everything in simple terms like this, I think I got through to the kitten. He sat up straight and asked me to teach him. Good. In the cat world, good manners are a must.

I was about to lead the orange tabby into an Intro to Hunting when Satoru said, "Oh! Look, Yoshimine. They've started playing together."

"Aren't they fighting?"

"No, Nana's going easy on him."

This isn't a game, folks, I'm teaching. Whatever.

"If they carry on together like this, maybe I can convince you to keep Nana for me."

Well, I'm doing my thing here, so you chaps keep doing whatever you're doing. Don't mind us.

Satoru watched as the orange tabby pounced on the toy mouse the way I taught him to, and his eyes narrowed into a smile.

"He's so excitable, just like the cat I used to have years ago."

You're right about that. When he's supposed to crouch quietly and blend in, he madly waves his tail around instead. I stretch my tail out smoothly, but this little kitten waves his around like a helicopter. And when he crouches down ready to pounce, he keeps his body way too high off the ground.

"What was Nana like when he was little?"

"I found him when he was a grown cat, so I don't know what sort of kitten he was. I wish I could have known him then. I'm sure he was adorable."

You're right there. My level of cuteness when I was a kitten was such that passersby vied for the privilege of leaving me a little something to eat.

"Now that you mention it ..." Yoshimine said, as if suddenly remembering something, "did you see that cat you adopted ever again?"

"Unfortunately, no. It died when I was in high school."

"I see," Yoshimine said, his voice respectfully mournful.

"I wish you could have seen him. Sorry about that. But I really didn't want the word to get back to my aunt."

Whoa there, Satoru. What on earth are you hinting at here?

I ordered the orange tabby to run through the exercises I'd taught him on his own, and turned my attention to Satoru and Yoshimine's conversation.

∽

Yoshimine's parents' divorce went through without a hitch, his father getting custody of their son. This was because Yoshimine wanted to live with his grandmother. It also meant he could avoid the inconvenience of changing his last name.

As if they had been set free, both his parents went off on overseas postings, and appeared to be doing well. And, as ever, Yoshimine found that living with his grandmother suited him down to the ground.

A year passed and, during the first semester of their last year in junior high, the class went on a school trip to Fukuoka.

Yoshimine realized that something was bothering Satoru

only after he'd found out what had happened on a previous
school trip—that Satoru's parents had died in an accident.

Satoru had looked glum from the moment they departed.
On their first day in Fukuoka, when they had some free time,
he was uncharacteristically quiet, even though he was with his
usual group of friends.

Yoshimine was concerned that the trip had tapped into
depressing memories, but with all the other students around
it was hard to find an opportunity to talk to him about it.

After dinner, when they were browsing through the souvenir shop in the hotel, he finally found his chance.

"Are you okay?"

Satoru looked worried. He glanced up at Yoshimine and
said in a low voice, "I was wondering if I can get to Kokura."

From Hakata Station in Fukuoka to Kokura was about
twenty minutes by the Shinkansen train. So of course it was
possible. But only if they weren't on a school trip. Which they
were.

Always alert to the dangers of the students wandering off,
the teachers chaperoning the trip had set up a tight surveillance
system. The daily activities were scheduled to the minute. After
checking into the hotel, it was strictly forbidden for students to
go out on their own. A teacher was always stationed at the
hotel entrance. If a student were to try to slip out to have fun at
night, there was a very real risk that they might be sent home.

So for Satoru to go to Kokura on his own was, in the circumstances, not an option. Yet the obedient, sharp-witted

Satoru wouldn't have said such a thing unless he had a very good reason.

"How come?" Yoshimine asked.

So Satoru told him.

It had to do with the cat he'd had back when his parents were still alive. When they died and his aunt took him in, he'd had to give up the cat, and relatives in Kokura had adopted it.

"My aunt's always so busy I can't ask her to take me to Kokura just to see the cat ... So I was wondering if, when we have a free moment during the day, I could slip away and go there to visit it."

"Do you really want to see the cat that much?"

"He's family," Satoru replied.

"I see," Yoshimine said, folding his arms. He'd never had a pet himself, and had no particular fondness for cats.

But for Satoru, that cat was something he and his parents had all loved, the one remaining family member from that happy time they shared before his parents died. It all made perfect sense.

Okay, then.

So it's just a cat, but it is, after all, a *cat*. For his friend, the one and only cat in the world.

"Let's do it."

But then Satoru hesitated. "Yeah, but ..." He trembled.

"We have three hours till lights-out. You know your relatives' address, don't you?"

It turned out to be in an apartment building not far from Kokura Station.

"If we skip having a bath, we'll have plenty of time. But you won't have a cent left to buy anything afterward."

A round trip to Kokura would cost several thousand yen.

"We can't tell anyone in our group. If they knew, then they could get into trouble, too. When it's time to go for a bath, we'll tell them we'll be down in a minute, and then we'll make our getaway."

"I'll go on my own. I don't want anyone else to get mixed up in this."

"Come on, mate. I'm your best friend." And with that, Yoshimine slapped him on the back.

They hadn't been allowed to bring any clothes other than their school uniform and pajamas, so the choice was between those. They'd both brought jerseys to wear in bed, so they opted for those, since they wouldn't stand out as much as school shirts and blazers.

When it came to their turn to go down to the bath, they pretended to need more time to get ready for it.

They waited three minutes, then left their room. They avoided the main entrance, because of the teacher standing guard, and headed straight to the emergency exit they had scouted out earlier. The doorknob on the fire exit had a plastic safety cover, which made it obvious if anyone used the door.

If a teacher found the cover missing, there would be an immediate roll call.

"What should we do?" Satoru asked anxiously. "The teachers will check this when they make their rounds."

"We go up," Yoshimine said, yanking him over to the elevators. "If we rip that cover off a door on another floor, they won't notice."

In order to isolate the noisy students from the other guests, all their rooms were adjacent. If they ripped the cover off the knob on a floor where only regular guests were staying, it was possible it would go undetected.

The hotel rooms started on the fifth floor, and they'd heard that students on school trips were always housed on the fifth, sixth and seventh floors. When they got out at the eighth floor the hallway was so quiet they couldn't believe how peaceful the hotel could be.

"Okay, let's go."

They yanked off the safety cover, pulled open the heavy fire door and hurtled down the stairs. Exiting on the ground floor, they reached a service entrance, through which they headed, trying to look nonchalant. Suddenly, a voice called out from behind them, "You there!"

Startled, they turned around and saw a hotel employee.

"Aren't you students on a school trip?"

Oh god, Yoshimine thought. The hotel employees must have been warned to keep an eye out for escapees.

"No, actually we're not!" Yoshimine shot back, starting for the door.

"Hold it right there!" the man shouted, heading after him.

"Run for it!"

Yoshimine darted off, Satoru chasing after him.

"Somebody stop those boys!"

The employee's shouts immediately led to more obstacles being put in their way, but, running this way and that, trying to avoid all the people who were joining the pursuit, they finally came to the hotel's main entrance.

Standing guard was the form teacher Yoshimine had met on his first day—the pretty woman who'd been so sympathetic.

"Yoshimine-kun! Satoru-kun! What are you doing?"

Satoru thought Yoshimine might give up at this point, but when Yoshimine shouted, "Let's go for it. Screw the consequences!" he sped up with his friend. The teacher raised her arms to stop them, but they slipped past her and leaped onto the crowded pavement outside the hotel, laughing all the way.

They might as well have used the main entrance to start with.

They kept on running, to shake off any pursuers, and Satoru shouted breathlessly at his friend, "Listen! Tell people I went out 'cause I was dying to go out at night and have some fun."

"Okay."

As they made their way down unfamiliar streets, they

asked for directions, and in about twenty minutes they had arrived at Hakata Station.

They were at the window for train tickets to Kokura when they heard someone calling from behind them.

"Hey! You boys!" It was a PE teacher, one of the chaperones.

They were escorted back to the hotel, called into one of the rooms where the teachers were staying and firmly scolded.

"Where on *earth* did you think you were going?"

They hadn't agreed on a story beforehand and weren't sure how to get through this. They glanced at each other, wondering who should go first.

"Satoru-kun." This from the kindly teacher. "Maybe being on a school trip was hard on you?"

Oh, the beautiful teacher, Miss Empathy. Well just stop it, Yoshimine thought. Drop the sympathy. Don't try to protect Satoru by bringing that up.

"No, that's not it," Satoru replied in an even voice, though his face had turned pale. "I just wanted to get out and have fun in the town. That's all."

"Don't lie to me. I know you're not that kind of boy."

Yoshimine nearly burst out laughing. What do *you* know about Satoru, Teacher?

Tell people I went out 'cause I was dying to go out at night and

have some fun. Satoru didn't want anyone to know he was trying to get to Kokura to see a cat.

"Satoru, I'm sorry. I've had enough."

Yoshimine looked as though he was about to give up. The
teachers' attention turned to him.

"It's my fault, ma'am. I was dying to eat some Nagahama
ramen. And I was asking for directions at the station.

"Thing is," he went on, "I had ramen at an outdoor stall
once in Tenjin with my parents, back before they got divorced.
Since we weren't far from there, I remembered my parents and
memories of those good times. Satoru just tagged along
with me."

Their circumstances were different, but both boys were no
longer with their parents. That was justification enough—two
lonely boys wanting to cheer each other up.

"Yoshimine …" Satoru was about to say something, but
Yoshimine cut him off. "It's okay," he said. He needed his
friend to keep quiet if he really didn't want the world to know
about his precious cat.

The teachers remained silent and stern, but they were
clearly uncertain how to proceed.

"I understand how you feel, but rules are rules. You can't
just go off on your own during a school trip," said the PE
teacher sourly.

They should have just bowed their heads and apologized
then and there. Both of their guardians were contacted and,
as an example to the rest of the students, their punishment

was to sit in the hallway, in uncomfortable formal *seiza* style, legs tucked under them, until late in the evening.

As soon as he got home from the trip, Yoshimine asked his grandmother a favor.

"Grandma, *please*, there's something I really, really need to ask of you."

He wanted his grandmother to call Satoru's aunt to apologize. To apologize for getting Satoru mixed up in all this.

His grandmother knew her grandson had never been to Tenjin with his parents, but she did as requested, no questions asked.

"I'm so sorry that Satoru-chan got yelled at because of what Daigo did."

Satoru's aunt seemed embarrassed. "I'm the one who should apologize," she said. "Yoshimine-kun wanted to abandon the idea but, apparently, Satoru dragged him along."

So that was how Satoru had explained things at home.

"I know you two wouldn't break the rules without a very good reason," Yoshimine's grandmother said later to him.

He felt choked.

This kind and considerate grandmother died some ten years ago, at a ripe old age.

Satoru had moved away when he graduated from junior high, but Yoshimine had continued to write to him, and when he told him of his grandmother's passing Satoru had come a long way to attend the funeral.

When he was thanked for attending, Satoru smiled. "She was my grandmother, too, wasn't she?" he said. Yoshimine nodded, his eyes filling with tears.

His father, who was in charge of the funeral, had no intention of taking over the farm, and placed the house and its land in the care of nearby relatives, who had already got used to farming the fields and rice paddies when Yoshimine's grandmother was no longer able to.

Yoshimine had proposed that he take over the farm, but was persuaded otherwise. Apparently, the farm wouldn't make him much money and it would cause him a lot of trouble when it came to finding a wife.

"Well, as my relatives predicted, no marriage prospects so far," Yoshimine told Satoru now.

"Well, if I were a woman, I would definitely be interested," Satoru said.

"If you know any women who share your values, be sure to introduce me to them."

Smiling, Yoshimine poured more *shochu* into his glass. Now that they had checked the fields for the evening, it was time for a couple of drinks with dinner.

Satoru had some beer with his, but later drank only barley tea. He had never been much of a drinker, and had recently become even less able to hold his liquor.

"I was hoping that before I leave tomorrow, I might pay a visit to your grandmother's grave," he said.

The grave was in the hills behind the house. In Yoshimine's small truck, it would take less than five minutes to get there.

To celebrate his friend's visit, Yoshimine had planned to stay up late with him, but with an early-to-bed-early-to-rise habit drilled into him, he didn't even make it to midnight.

∽

Satoru and Yoshimine went out first thing in the morning in Yoshimine's truck, talking as they drove about the night before.

Perfect, I thought. I have my own little something to take care of while they're gone.

Hey, orange tabby. Yes. *You.*

You remember what I taught you yesterday, don't you? We're going to go over how to handle yourself in a fight.

I crinkled up my nose and flattened my ears back. Okay, when you see an angry cat like this, what do you do?

The orange tabby followed suit, crinkling up his nose, laying his ears back, arching his back and making the fur on his back and tail stand on end.

Excellent. Well done.

Now, the final test. When I make an angry face, instantly strike a fighting pose. Impress Yoshimine. Listen, we need to have this nailed before I leave. So keep on your toes.

The orange tabby was full of spirit. Just then, Satoru and Yoshimine came back.

Timing it perfectly, so they were just coming into the room, I signaled to the orange tabby to adopt a fighting stance.

The kitten puffed up the fur all over his body like an exploding ball of wool. He was determined to show Yoshimine his best stance.

"*What the—?!*" Satoru sounded totally confused. "They were getting on so well yesterday. I wonder what's happened all of a sudden."

Who knows? Kittens are pretty impulsive. Perhaps he changed his mind?

"Maybe he's already forgotten about yesterday." Yoshimine looked puzzled, too.

"Well, let's see how it goes for a while. He might just be in a bad mood."

Satoru was planning to leave in the morning, but held off until the afternoon. He tried out a few things, including putting the kitten and me in separate rooms for a while.

Unfortunately the kitten continued performing until we left. Every time I urged him on, he took up his best fighting pose. He was really into it, for a kitten. If he kept this up, he might actually make something of himself.

"Why don't you leave Nana here and see how it goes? Give him a few days and they might get used to each other," suggested Yoshimine when he got back from his morning farm chores.

"I don't think so," Satoru said doubtfully. "Nana got furious and hid in his basket, so it doesn't look promising. It's too bad, but if they don't get on, forcing them to be together is sort of cruel."

"Really? That's too bad. He's such a good cat."

Yoshimine, I don't dislike you, so don't think badly of me, okay?

But I'm still not ready to leave that silver van for good.

Satoru still seemed a bit sad about the whole thing, but with the little orange tabby looking so angry, wearing that ominous look, he finally gave up on the idea. Holding my basket to his chest, he climbed into the silver van.

"It really is a shame."

"You say that, but you look pretty happy about the whole thing."

To Yoshimine's teasing, Satoru gave only a "Hmm" in reply. His remark seemed to have hit the nail on the head. "Well ..." he went on, "it's true I'm going to find it hard to part with Nana."

"If you like him so much, why do you have to give him away?"

Oh. You threw that pitch right down the middle, didn't you, Yoshimine? A straight pitch, just like when you stuck your hand inside my basket when we first met.

Satoru looked perplexed and didn't reply.

"Never mind," Yoshimine said, not pressing the point. "If you ever have any trouble, come round, okay? I may not have any marriage prospects or savings, but one thing is certain—farmers never lack for food."

"But you see how Chatran and Nana are."

"They're not going to kill each other, and if it comes to that, we can just force them to live together even if they don't want to. They're just animals, you really don't need to worry so much about whether they get on."

"That's absurd. When animals are under too much stress, their fur can fall out."

"If it really doesn't work out, then I'll set it up so you can stay in one of the unoccupied houses in the village. People are afraid their houses will deteriorate so they want someone to live in them. The village is doing its best to attract young people to come here from the city, too."

"Thank you." Satoru smiled, but his voice was still a bit shaky. "If I really can't find a solution, then I'll definitely take you up on that."

"Good. I'll look forward to it."

Satoru and Yoshimine shook hands firmly.

"Thank you for everything. I'm pleased I was able to pay a visit to your grandmother's grave."

He got into the van, but just before he started the engine Satoru said, "Oh, that's right," and rolled down the window. "Yoshimine, do you remember the name of that cat I used to have?"

Yoshimine shook his head.

"He was called Hachi. He looked just like Nana, right down to the marks on his face like the Chinese character for eight. And Nana got his name because his tail looks like the character for seven."

Yoshimine burst out laughing. "You said Chatran's name was kind of corny, but the names you come up with are cheesy, too."

"One names them according to the way they look, and the other is into clichés. I'd say it's a tie."

Satoru beeped his horn lightly and drove off down the lane.

Y ou shouldn't act up like that, Nana, getting all upset over a little kitten."

Ahem. You said you were going to leave me there, but do you really think that's gonna fly?

"I am a little relieved, though. That we can go home together."

This I already knew.

"Like I promised, do you want to stop by the sea on the way back?"

Sounds great! I wonder how many of the delicacies in my usual gourmet seafood blend are really in there?

So the silver van headed toward the beach. Too much bother to stay in the basket, so I balanced on Satoru's lap as we bumped down the rough lane toward the sea.

When we got out of the van, Satoru scooped me up and hoofed it down the slope that led to the shore, but me, I clung on for dear life.

"Hey, Nana. What are you doing with your claws? It hurts!"

No way. *No. Way.* What is that *rushing* sound? I've never heard anything like it! What *is* it, that monstrous roar?

And there it was. The sea—spread out before my very eyes. An endless expanse of water rolling relentlessly toward us.

"Look, Nana. The sea. Aren't the waves fabulous?"

Fabulous?! What are you talking about? How optimistic humans can be, to think that this enormous mass of rolling water, this soaring energy—is *fabulous*?! I don't know about humans, but if any cat got caught up in it, that would be the end of it, for sure!

"Let's go down by the water's edge."

NO. WAY.

"Nana! Ouch! That hurts!"

I slipped out of Satoru's arms, struggled to grasp higher ground, and leaped right up on top of his head, where, I have to admit, there wasn't much hair.

"Your claws! Nana, don't scratch me with your claws!"

This is no good. I need a safer place than Satoru's head! Humph!

I pushed off and landed on all fours on the ground. Then, scuttling as fast as I could, I dashed in the opposite direction from the shoreline.

"Nana!"

I ran straight up onto a nearby bluff and settled down at the base of a pine tree growing at an angle from the bare rock.

"Why do you have to go all the way up there? Come down here!"

Not gonna happen. If I'm not careful, I'll get swept away by a wave and die!

"Come on down from there, Nana. It's too hard for me to climb up!"

In the end, Satoru, with great care and awkwardness, clambered up the bluff to rescue me.

From my first experience of the sea, I learned a valuable lesson.

The sea is where you go to reminisce when you are far away from home.

Delicacies of the sea are not something cats should catch by themselves. It's quite acceptable to allow humans to prepare them for us.

"My scalp is full of scratches. It's going to sting when I shampoo, that's for sure."

Satoru muttered a couple more complaints, but then gave a little chuckle.

"But you know, I never imagined you'd be that afraid of the sea. I've seen a side of you I've never witnessed before, but it's good to know you don't like it."

I do like it, viewed from a distance. The sea, that is.

The van drove smoothly along the shoreline. I gazed at the glittering dark-blue water, my tail happily raised to the sky.

Until then, my life had been limited to the modest territory of Satoru's apartment and a small area around it. A decent-sized territory for a cat, really, but pretty modest compared to the vastness of this world.

A cat could never see all the sights the world has to offer in one lifetime. There's just so much out there.

Satoru?

Since we had embarked on our journey, I'd seen the town where you spent your childhood. And a farming village. And the sea.

I wondered what new scenes we would see together before this journey was over.

3

Sugi and Chikako's Hotel for Pets

Relax with your beloved pet while enjoying a breathtaking view of Mount Fuji.

This was the slogan with which Shusuke Sugi and his wife Chikako launched their bed and breakfast three years ago.

The whole thing came about when the company Sugi worked for started to struggle and began to explore the idea of voluntary redundancy. Around that time, a B&B next to the fruit orchards owned by Chikako's parents came up for sale at a greatly reduced price, and the couple bought it, lock, stock and barrel, and opened it up for business. They considered part of its appeal would be to offer a discount to guests wanting to do pick-your-own in the orchards next door. This worked both ways, for it would benefit the orchard business to have customers referred to them, which was another reason they decided to take the plunge.

In the end, though, the B&B's biggest selling point was that they allowed pets.

It was Chikako who came up with the idea.

Using the first and second floors, plus a small cottage on the grounds, they were able to lodge guests with dogs or cats separately. Dogs and cats each had their own floor and, as long as they got on with their own kind, they could enjoy life off the lead or outside their basket. Issues of compatibility were left to the owners' discretion.

Very few B&Bs in the area allowed both dogs and cats; most places catered just for dogs. Some of the larger inns accepted both, but most of them demanded that pets remain on a lead or in a basket.

Sugi was more of a dog person, so at first he wasn't sure about his wife's idea, but after the B&B had been running for three years he had to admit she'd been very perceptive.

In addition to Chikako's family business, there were plenty of other orchards and wineries nearby, and within their prefecture this area attracted a lot of tourists—but a B&B where cats could stay, stress-free, was almost unheard of. Word of mouth and repeat business led to an increase in cat-owning guests, and these days, guests with cats outnumbered those with dogs.

Chikako loved all cats, and cat-owning guests always received a warm welcome, but she'd never been happier than with the guests who were arriving today.

Chikako had been on the second floor making the bed in the sunniest twin room and now, dirty linen in hand and humming a tune, she made her way downstairs.

"You seem pretty upbeat," Sugi said. He'd tried to make it sound casual, but it came out sounding oddly churlish. Chikako looked at him, puzzled.

"Aren't you happy? Satoru Miyawaki is bringing his cat for the very first time."

"Of course I am, but ..." Sugi said hurriedly, trying to gloss it over. "I was just wondering if his cat will get on with our pets."

Their own pets were a dog—a Kai Ken breed—and a brown tabby cat. The Kai Ken was a three-year-old male named Toramaru, while the brown tabby cat was a twelve-year-old female named Momo. Toramaru (*tora* meaning "tiger") got his name from the distinctive orangey brindle fur that certain Kai Ken dogs have, while Momo, which means "peach," was named after the main crop of the orchard.

"Don't worry so much. It'll be fine. Our little ones are used to having guests."

Sugi persisted, despite Chikako's teasing smile. "Satoru is giving away his cat, you know. I'm sure he can't be too happy about that."

The man they were expecting was their mutual high-school friend Satoru Miyawaki.

An e-mail had arrived in Sugi's inbox saying that, though Satoru loved his cat very much, there was a compelling reason why he couldn't keep him any longer, and he was looking for someone to take care of him.

No explanation of what this *compelling reason* was, but when Sugi noticed in the newspaper that a large corporation had started to lay off employees, he didn't pursue the matter.

Satoru's company, as he recalled, was a subsidiary of that corporation.

If an organization that big is beginning to lay people off,
Sugi pondered, then I guess it's only to be expected that my
old company would do the same. He was lucky to have left his
local firm when he did.

"But if we take on his cat, we can give him back at any
time, can't we?" Chikako said, and laughed. "I'm thinking of
it more as a temporary arrangement. I'll take good care of him
while we have him, of course. That goes without saying."

A temporary arrangement. Sugi hadn't considered that.
Chikako was always so positive and forward-thinking. Always looking on the bright side. Calling Sugi *prudent* made it
sound positive, but the fact was he tended to be far less optimistic, the exact opposite of Chikako.

"There really must be some sound reason for him to give
away his cat all of a sudden … But one day, I know, Satoru
will come back for him."

Chikako seemed to believe categorically that Satoru's love
for his cat would overcome all obstacles. When it came to cat
love, the two of them had always been on the same wavelength.

Bed linen in hand, Chikako went into the laundry room.
"Get down, Momo." Their cat seemed to be asleep on top of
the washing machine. "Satoru says his cat is named Nana.
Make sure you get on with him now." Chikako sounded like
she was singing as she said this. "Oh!" she called loudly. "Darling, make sure you tell Tora the same thing."

Both dog and cat were equally important to them, but, in practical terms, there was a clear division of duties. Chikako, the cat person, was in charge of Momo, while Sugi, more on the dog side of the divide, handled all things Toramaru.

Whenever there's anything major happening in our family we need to inform both our dog and cat—this proposal by Chikako had become a firm family rule.

Sugi slipped his feet into the sandals he had left at the entrance and went outside. When the weather was fine, during the day they let Toramaru have free run of a special fenced-off space in the front yard. Sugi's father-in-law, who prided himself on his carpentry skills, had built a kennel for Toramaru.

"Tora!"

Hearing his name, Tora wagged his curled tail energetically and leaped up to his owner. He could jump so high it looked like he might one day bound over the high fence, so, to be on the safe side, whenever guests arrived, they put him on a lead tied to his kennel. The expert who had given them the dog told them how the breed divided into two types—the slimmer types who were built for chasing deer, and the thicker-set types who were good at chasing wild boar. Toramaru was a textbook deer type.

For two days, Satoru would be the only guest, so Sugi had let Tora off his lead.

"Satoru is coming this evening. The friend I told you about."

Sugi had acquired Toramaru three years earlier when they

first opened the B&B, but right about that time, Satoru was moved over to a busy section of his company and had little free time to visit him and Chikako. Sugi had been able to see him occasionally when he went into Tokyo to purchase food for the B&B, but it would be the first time in three years that Chikako had seen him, and the very first time for Toramaru.

Satoru had always seemed very busy with work, so Sugi presumed his job must be secure, but with staffing cutbacks there could be many factors at play.

"This is the first time you'll meet Satoru and Nana, Tora, and I hope you'll get on with them."

Sugi gave Toramaru's head a brisk rub, and the dog gave a throaty growl. Rough stroking like this was one of the real pleasures of having a dog. If he tried the same with Momo, he thought, she'd probably lunge at him, claws bared.

"You be on your best behavior, okay?"

Toramaru looked searchingly into Sugi's eyes, then gave another husky growl.

That day, there was no doves-about-to-pop-out kind of music playing in the silver van.

Perhaps thinking he'd have a break from the car stereo, Satoru had the radio on instead. A little while ago, a refined-sounding older gentleman had been enthusiastically introducing a book on some program or other. Apparently, he was an actor.

He talked elegantly, yet occasionally he would use unexpected language: words like "cool" and "awesome," and even for a mere cat like myself, hearing this gentleman rattle on and on about how *awesome* a book was really made me smile.

All well and good, but no matter how appealing a book might be, I can't read it. As I explained earlier, most animals are multilingual when it comes to listening, but reading is beyond us. Reading and writing seem to belong to a special linguistic system that only humans possess.

"Hmm, if Mr. Kodama, the host of the program, likes the book so much, maybe I should read it," Satoru murmured. When he was at home, he spent more time reading books than watching TV; he'd even been known to shed the occasional tear as he turned the pages. If he ever caught me watching him during one of these moments, he would look embarrassed and say, "Stop staring."

The book program came to an end, and after a while a nursery song began to play.

Put your head above the clouds, look down on all the other mountains around . . .

Sometimes it's nice to hear this kind of gentle singing. Though the melody was making me sleepy.

Hear the thunder roll above . . .
Mount Fuji is the highest mountain in all of Japan . . .

Hm? At this last line, I sat up, rested my paws on the passenger-seat window and craned my neck to see out.

For a while now, there had been a huge triangular mountain plonked down in the distance.

"Oh, did you make the connection, Nana?"

Humans always underestimate our language skills. Just 'cause they can read and write, there's no need to act all high and mighty.

"That's right, it's a song about Mount Fuji. Great timing, don't you think?"

When that triangular-shaped mountain, with its base spread so wide, loomed closer, Satoru said, "That's Mount Fuji."

On TV and in photos, it looks just like a triangle that has flopped down onto the earth, but when you see it in real life it feels overwhelming, like it's closing in on you.

It's the highest mountain in Japan at 3,776 meters, and there's even a mnemonic device for people to remember the elevation: Let's all be like Fuji-san, *Fuji-san no yo ni mi* [three] *na* [seven] *ni na* [seven] *rou* [six]—there are many higher mountains around the world, but as a free-standing single mountain it's unusually high. Satoru rattled on and on, explaining all kinds of facts in great detail.

I get it, how great it is. You don't need to go on and on. It makes total sense why there is a song dedicated to it. Yada yada.

You really have to see it with your own eyes, though. If you've only seen it on TV or in photos, it'll always remain just a triangular mountain sitting there. Like it was to me until right this moment.

Being big has its advantages. Just as being a big cat makes it easier to get by in life.

Still, this mountain *was* pretty darn amazing.

I wonder how many cats in Japan have seen the actual Mount Fuji. Unless they live around here, there can't be too many.

Our silver van was like a magic carriage. Every time I got into it, it carried me to a place I'd never been before.

At that moment, we were without doubt the greatest travelers in the world. And I was the world's greatest traveling cat.

The van veered off the main road and drove into a thick, lush forest.

The branches of the trees on either side had bunches of white paper bags hanging from them, apparently to protect the peaches growing on them—to keep the insects off and help the fruit ripen.

After zigzagging for quite some time, finally a large white house appeared in front of us.

"We're here, Nana."

This must be the bed and breakfast Satoru had talked about—the inn, run by some friends, that accepts pets. Today, the place was reserved just for us.

As the van pulled into a parking lot big enough for about ten cars, a man Satoru's age came out to greet us.

"Sugi!"

Satoru gave him a wave and unloaded his bag from the van.

"Is this your only bag? I'll help you."

"Apart from Nana, I only brought a change of clothes, as it's just the one night."

Sugi took hold of his friend's bag, and Satoru carried me in my basket, and together they climbed the gentle slope to the B&B entrance.

"What a wonderful place this is. Is that a dog run?"

On the way up the slope was a fairly large fenced-in space with what looked like a kennel near the back.

"I wanted a space where my dog could run free."

"A Kai Ken, isn't it? I remember you saying you had one."

From inside the basket, I sniffed at the air. A disgusting smell that belonged to that perennial rival to cats.

I squinted through the bars and watched as a hard-faced brindle dog sprang to his feet and stared challengingly in my direction.

"Yeah, his name is Toramaru."

"Is he okay living with a cat?"

"Of course. We have Momo, you know. And lots of guests bring their cats."

"Ah, that's right …"

I'd already heard from Satoru that they had a middle-aged female cat named Momo. She was twice my age, he'd said. I was still fairly young, so would we get on?

"Hey there. Hello. Glad to meet you, Toramaru," called Satoru, holding his hand over the fence.

Hold on a minute! Don't go speaking to that dog! I glowered from inside my basket.

This Kai Ken who went by the name of Toramaru cast a sharp glance our way and growled and bared his yellow teeth.

"Is he in a bad mood then?"

The instant Satoru inclined his head—*ruff!*—the dog barked at him.

"Whoa!"

As you might expect, Satoru quickly pulled his hand back from the fence.

Hey! Knock it off, hound!

Every single hair on my body was now standing on end.

If you're going to pick a fight with Satoru, then I—a cat with a strong sense of pride—am not going to just sit here and take it! If you don't want that nose of yours cut to shreds, then apologize right this instant, you mangy mutt!

"*Tora!*"

Sugi scolded him, but the mutt didn't stop his miserable yammering.

Satoru tried to soothe me, too.

"It's okay, Nana. Just hang in there."

He was holding the door of the basket closed from the outside because he knew I was quite willing to have it out with that stupid dog if I had to.

"I'm really sorry," Sugi said. "He's not usually like this."

"No, it's okay … I wonder if we did something to upset him."

"What's going on?" A woman hurried out of the front door. A pretty woman wearing an apron. "Is Tora angry?"

"It's no big deal. Hi, Chikako. How are you?" This from Satoru, who waved his hand at the woman.

"Satoru! I'm so sorry. Is everything all right?"

"No worries. I'm not used to cats or dogs getting angry with me, and it startled me for a second."

That's true. From an animal's point of view, Satoru was a pretty stress-free human, the kind that passing dogs and cats found no reason to pick a fight with.

An impudent dog like this leaping out at him was definitely a first.

"I'm so sorry. I really am," Sugi apologized, making another *knock it off* gesture at the dog. Toramaru let his curled tail droop. Serves you right, you stupid hound.

"It's fine. Really," Satoru said, trying to smooth things over. "He seems like a good, dependable dog. Maybe I look a little dodgy to him?"

Satoru tried again, reaching over the fence to scratch the dog's neck. The mutt quietly allowed him to stroke him, but it was obvious to me he was still sulking. Try flashing those gnashers at Satoru again for even a split second, mate, and you'll have *me* to deal with!

Through the bars, the dog and I exchanged some seething, hostile looks, but Satoru was then shown inside the house, so there was an unavoidable pause in the action.

We were shown a lovely sunny room on the second floor.

"After you get settled, come down," Chikako-san said. She turned and went nimbly down the stairs.

Well, I'll take a look around the room, then. I easily unlatched the door of the basket from the inside and slipped silently out. The neat little room had wooden flooring, and from a feline point of view looked perfectly cozy.

"Oh, hello there, Momo."

At the sound of Satoru's voice, I spun around to face the doorway. A small, dignified, brown female tabby was sitting quietly in the corner. Double my age, but still quite limber, from the look of things.

Nice to make your acquaintance, Momo greeted me, in a dignified voice quite in keeping with a dignified tabby. I hear you and Toramaru have already squabbled.

I let out a sniff. That dog has no manners. Baring his teeth at humans who try to say hello to him—he couldn't have been well brought up.

I was thoroughly sarcastic in my comments, and Momo smiled wryly.

Please forgive him. Just as your master is precious to you, so Toramaru's master is precious to him.

Your master is precious to you so you bark at your master's *friend*? That doesn't compute. *At all.*

As if sensing my displeasure Momo gave another wry smile.

I'm really sorry. I believe our master is not quite as strong a character as your master.

I still didn't get it. I refrained from objecting, though, because I didn't want to be disrespectful to an older lady.

∽

"H e seems to be getting on well with Momo."
Satoru had come down to the lobby-cum-lounge and, with a smile, he was pointing upstairs.

"They're in the bedroom, getting to know each other better. Now, if only Toramaru could be friendlier. Maybe he's angry that I brought a cat along?"

"He should be used to guests bringing cats by now." Chikako tilted her head, puzzled, and offered them some herbal tea.

"Darling, you did explain things to Toramaru, didn't you?" Chikako scolded Sugi jokingly.

"Of course I did," Sugi pouted, his tone a little snappy.

You be on your best behavior, okay? Sugi had said, as Toramaru gazed into his eyes. So why did he then bark at Satoru?

Maybe Toramaru had detected some discomfort in Sugi?

"Wow, this is delicious," Satoru said as he sipped his tea, and Chikako beamed.

"I'm so happy! Our guests seem to like it, too. The herbs are from our garden." Chikako looked over at Sugi sternly. "The first time I made herbal tea for him, he said it was like drinking toothpaste."

One silly slip of the tongue back when they had first got

married, and Chikako still bore a grudge. Thinking about this, Sugi had often wished he could follow Satoru's lead and be shrewder in dealing with things. But, in truth, Sugi found openly praising anyone a bit embarrassing.

"It's slightly sweet. What do you put in it?" Satoru asked.

"Stevia."

"Ah, that makes sense."

"This is why I enjoy talking to Satoru, because we can talk about things like this!"

"Your business seems to be doing well," Satoru said, clearing his throat.

"It is. Targeting guests with cats was a smart move," Sugi said.

"All *my* idea," Chikako returned.

"Indeed. Entirely the wife's doing," Sugi added. "But what about you? Are *you* doing okay? Giving away your cat ... all of a sudden?"

Sugi had found it hard to ask this question in an e-mail, so he had planned to do it when they were face to face.

"Yeah, well ... you know ..." Satoru gave a troubled smile, and when he did, he suddenly looked very old.

"I heard the business group your company belongs to has started to lay people off."

"It's not really that ... There are other things involved."

Chikako gave Sugi a stealthy wink to signal him to stop. *Okay*, he signaled back.

"I was so relieved when you said you'd take Nana for me.

I've asked quite a few people now, and taken Nana to see them, but somehow it just hasn't worked out."

"There's one thing I'd like to say upfront, Satoru," Chikako said, sitting up straight. "We're thinking of it as temporary. We'll take good care of Nana, of course, but if things work out for you so you can take him again, we'll have no problem if you come back for him, anytime."

Satoru looked as though this had really struck a chord, and for a moment he pursed his lips and looked at his feet.

That face—lips pursed, trying his best to keep his feelings in check—was one both Chikako and Sugi had seen before.

Suddenly Satoru looked up and smiled.

"Thank you. I'm sorry to be so selfish, but it really makes me happy to hear that."

⌒

Satoru had become a mutual friend, but Sugi had been the first one to form a bond with him.

In the spring of their first year in high school, the three of them were all in the same class.

In their new form room, students from their previous junior high tended to group together, weighing up the situation, wondering who to make friends with. Satoru wasn't hanging out with anyone. There didn't seem to be anyone else from the school he had just come from.

They learned later that he'd arrived from another prefecture during the spring holidays and had taken the transfer exam, which was why he didn't know a soul.

It was during one of the periodic exams that they became friends.

Sugi had crammed all night for the exam, and his head was stuffed with mathematical equations and English vocabulary. He was on his bike, heading to school, pedaling as gently as he could, in case some unexpected jolt or vibration drove all the facts he'd memorized from his brain.

Along the road to school, he spied a face he knew. That looks like Satoru from my class, he thought, as he drew closer. Satoru had got off his bike and was standing beside a wide ditch.

The ditch was the width of a stream, an agricultural irrigation channel lined with concrete on both sides, about as deep as a child was tall. Satoru was staring down at it, a serious look on his face.

Sugi wondered what he was up to, but didn't have much time to spare before school started. Their eyes had met, so he thought he'd just give him a nod and pass on by, but he began to feel that that would make things awkward later, so after he'd gone on a little bit, he stopped.

"What're you doing?" Sugi asked.

Satoru looked over at him, as if surprised. He must have thought Sugi would just cycle by.

"Um, I found something a little troubling, that's all."

Satoru pointed down at the ditch, where Sugi could now see a small dog shivering. The dog had managed to scramble on top of a tiny sandbar where gravel and dirt had piled up, and his thick white-and-brown fur was soaked and plastered to him.

"It's a Shih Tzu."

Sugi knew the breed, because Chikako's family had one. They ran a fruit orchard, loved animals, and ever since she was a young child they'd had several dogs and cats, which was something that drew customers in. And Sugi had always envied their attitude to animals.

Sugi's family lived in company housing; his father was a middle-management company employee, and because of his mother's allergies, the only pets she would allow were hairless ones such as goldfish or turtles. His dream had always been to have a dog, but this was never going to happen in his own house, so being with Chikako's family at least came close.

"He must have fallen in."

"I guess so," Satoru said, nodding. There were no steps down to the ditch that they could see.

"He's not the type of dog you'd expect to be a stray, so I reckon he must have wandered away from his home and got lost ..."

At Chikako's, during the day they let their dogs run free in the orchards so the customers who came to pick fruit could enjoy their company, but at night they always made sure they were brought inside the house.

"Go on ahead. You don't need to stick around," Satoru urged him, but for Sugi it was a delicate decision. If it emerged later that he'd ignored a poor little dog that had fallen into a ditch, then Chikako would be pretty upset.

"Yeah, but I'm worried about him."

Glancing at his watch, Sugi got off his bike. He was going to be late for school, but if he got there before first period he'd still be able to take the exam.

"Let's sort this out as quickly as we can."

Satoru smiled. "You're a good guy, Sugi."

All he'd been worried about was Chikako's reaction, and he found this praise from Satoru embarrassing.

"If we go down there, our ankles will get soaked."

The sandbar where the Shih Tzu was standing was too far away to leap to from either side of the ditch. The water was full of algae and grass so they couldn't see the bottom, and they were reluctant to take their shoes off in case there were any pieces of glass.

Sugi noticed a pile of boards left on the side of the road, the remnants, perhaps, of some scaffolding. He ran over and pulled one out.

"If we angle it down near the dog, he might be able to use it as a bridge and climb along it."

"Maybe."

But even with the board right in front of it, the Shih Tzu didn't react.

They tried calling, but the dog just stood there trembling, not taking a single step.

"Maybe it can't see it," Satoru said, a serious look on his

face. "If you look at him closely from the side, his eyes are a bit cloudy. He might be getting cataracts."

It was hard to tell the age of the baby-faced dog, but its coat was definitely a bit worn.

"Amazing that the little guy made it this far!"

There was a busy motorway nearby; it was a miracle the dog hadn't been run over. Perhaps it had fallen into the ditch because it couldn't see properly.

"I'm going to go down. If I use this, I won't get wet." Satoru put a foot on the board they'd stretched out toward the dog.

"Be careful, it's dangerous."

The board was old and weathered. It might not even hold a dog's weight, let alone that of a high-school boy. Just as these thoughts were going through Sugi's head, the board let out an ominous creak.

"Whoa!"

Satoru swayed on the board, and in an instant, it had split completely in two and collapsed into the ditch. There was a loud splash and a spray of water as Satoru landed on his rear in the ankle-deep stream.

Woof woof woof. The Shih Tzu barked, and started to splash his way blindly through the water.

"Wa-wait!"

Satoru scrambled to his feet and tried to follow him. But his splashing only scared the Shih Tzu even more, and he didn't stop. You wouldn't know he was old and half blind, the way the dog tore through the water.

"I'll run ahead and climb down! We'll catch him. Don't let him get away!"

Sugi hared down the road, past the fleeing Shih Tzu, and took a flying leap into the ditch.

There was an explosion of water. The Shih Tzu leaped into the air and screeched to a halt. Then he spun around and started to race back the way he had come.

"He's coming back your way. Grab him!"

Satoru leaped toward the dog like a goalie. The Shih Tzu made a tight turn, trying to slip past, but Satoru managed to snag a hind leg. Panicked, the dog chomped down on his hand.

"Ow!"

"Hang on! Don't let go!"

Sugi whipped off his blazer, threw it over the Shih Tzu and grabbed him. Swaddled, the dog finally gave up his struggle.

"You okay?" Sugi asked.

Satoru smiled wryly. "This could be pretty serious," he said, showing his hand. Spots of blood were bubbling up. For such a little creature, the dog certainly knew how to bite.

"You'd better get to the hospital."

No chance I'll make that exam now, Sugi thought.

They took the dog to a police station beside the motorway, but when they went to the hospital there was a problem. Satoru didn't have an insurance card. Being high-school students, they didn't have enough cash either, so they ended up handing over their school ID cards and promising to come back and pay—and finally Satoru was treated.

By the time they got to school, second period was just finishing.

They went to the faculty office and explained to their form teacher what had happened. The whole thing sounded like a joke, but Satoru's resemblance to a drowned rat, and his bandaged hand, must have convinced her, for the teacher accepted their version of events.

"What happened to you guys?" asked Chikako, playing the concerned older sister as the boys returned to the classroom.

When she heard about the rescued Shih Tzu, she wanted to see him, so they stopped at the police station on their way home from school. Satoru was concerned about the dog, too, so the three of them went together.

The old Shih Tzu with his cloudy eyes was on a lead in the corner of the lobby, bowls of dry dog biscuits and water next to it. No one had reported a missing dog.

"He really is quite old. I don't think he can see well at all." Chikako knelt down in front of the dog and waved her hand in front of his eyes. The Shih Tzu was slow to react.

"I was wondering if we could ask you to take him," said a middle-aged police officer. "Looking after lost dogs isn't really a policeman's job, so we can't keep him here for very long."

"If you can't keep him here ... then what will happen to him?" Satoru asked.

The officer tilted his head. "If the owner doesn't appear in the next few days, he'll go to the pound."

"How could you!" Chikako snapped. "You know they'll put him down! If the owner doesn't turn up in time—"

Satoru, pale and silent, nudged Sugi in the ribs. "How about keeping it at your place?" he suggested. Instead of arguing with the officer, Satoru seemed to be looking for a practical solution.

"No can do. My mom is allergic to any animal with fur. What about yours, Satoru?"

"We're in company housing and they don't allow pets."

Chikako, who was still carping at the police officer, turned around. "It's okay," she said. "We'll keep him at ours."

"Are you sure you can make that decision right now? Shouldn't you ask your parents or something?"

Satoru seemed alarmed by her snap decision, but Chikako just glared at him in irritation.

"Well, we can't just leave him here!"

Chikako called home from the payphone in the lobby. Almost an hour later, her father pulled up at the station in his small truck. They loaded her bike onto the truck bed, and Chikako got into the passenger seat and held the Shih Tzu on her lap.

"Okay, see you soon!" she called. "Satoru, if you're worried about him, you can come and visit him at my place!"

"Ah—thanks."

Satoru seemed a bit intimidated by Chikako's forceful manner.

Then Chikako was gone, like a storm departing, and the boys burst out laughing.

"That Sakita-san is really something."

"She sure is. She's always had strong views when it comes to animals, ever since she was little."

"Have you known her since she was a kid?" Satoru wanted to know.

"We're childhood friends," Sugi explained.

"I get it," Satoru said, nodding. "So that's why Sakita-san calls you Shu-chan?"

"I told her to drop that."

"What's wrong with it? She's your cute, dependable childhood friend."

The way he'd casually called her *cute* startled Sugi. Chikako was spirited, kind and, yes, cute. He'd always known that. Still, Sugi had never spoken about these things out loud.

It made him feel like he'd lost out.

"But will her family really be okay about taking in an unknown dog without any warning?" Satoru asked.

"It'll be fine. Her family are mad about animals. They have five or six dogs and cats already."

"Really? Cats, too?"

"Chikako's more of a cat person."

"I see," Satoru said, smiling. "I love cats, too. I wouldn't mind making sure the Shih Tzu's okay, but it would be nice to see her cats, too."

Sugi was hit by another wave of anxiety. It was clear Satoru and Chikako were going to get on well.

That evening, Chikako phoned Sugi. The fact that he had missed taking the exam in order to rescue the dog had made an impression on her.

"By the way," she asked, "which one of you found it?"

Sugi wished he'd been the one who'd come across the dog—the thought of saying this had crossed his mind. *But if I had, I probably would have just let him be. Perhaps the most I would have done would have been to check on him on the way home.*

"Well, we were both passing at about the same time."

A little white lie.

"But I think Satoru actually spotted him first," he added hastily.

"We haven't spoken much up till now, but Satoru's a pretty good guy."

Chikako seemed to like Satoru a lot. He had known she would.

The three of them often talked together after this. And Satoru and Sugi often went to Chikako's house to see how the Shih Tzu was settling in.

Whenever Sugi went to see Chikako, he'd be put to work helping out in the orchards, as would Satoru. From the way he spoke, Satoru seemed like a real city boy, but he was, surprisingly, used to farm work, and Chikako's family quickly grew fond of him.

The stray Shih Tzu's owner never did materialize, so the Sakita family ended up keeping him permanently. Satoru felt bad about it and said he'd try to find somebody to take the dog, but Chikako waved this away.

The younger Shih Tzu they already had got on with the new one—they were like parent and child—and, typically for Chikako, she referred to the latter as "the Shih Tzu Miyawaki gave us."

The cats at the Sakitas' were friendlier to Satoru than to Sugi. They had, from the start, sensed that Sugi was more of a dog person. Things evened out, though, since the dogs were much friendlier to him than to Satoru. "The Shih Tzu Miyawaki gave us," perhaps remembering how Satoru had been the one to chase him down, was friendlier to Sugi than to Satoru, who had found him.

One day at school, Satoru was leafing through the part-time jobs listings in the newspaper. The end-of-term exams were approaching, and their teachers had joked with them not to pick up any more stray dogs.

"Are you looking for a holiday job?" Sugi asked.

"Yeah … I was wondering if there're any with a decent hourly rate."

"How come? Isn't your allowance enough?"

"No, it's just that I want to take a trip during the summer holiday, and I'd like to go as soon as possible."

"Where to?"

"Kokura."

Sugi didn't know the place.

"It's in Fukuoka prefecture. Just before Hakata," Satoru explained.

Sugi knew exactly where he meant, but couldn't understand why Satoru would want to go there, instead of to Hakata, which was much larger.

"I have some distant relatives there," Satoru explained. "They took in our cat when we couldn't have him anymore. I haven't been to see him at all since then."

I see, Sugi thought. It's not Kokura he wants to visit, but a cat.

"Why couldn't you keep it?"

He asked this casually, but Satoru gave a troubled smile. He seemed unsure how to respond, and Sugi was just thinking that maybe he should change the subject when a shadow loomed over them.

"I heard, I heard." Laughing her usual audacious laugh, it was Chikako.

"Man, you're always sticking your nose into things, aren't you?" Sugi teased her.

"Shut it," she shot back. "I know exactly how you feel— wanting to visit your beloved cat. I'll pitch in and help!"

"Do you know where I can get work?" Satoru asked.

"And where you can begin this very weekend!" Chikako answered.

"Really? If there's a job that good, then tell me about it, too." Sugi had been starting to think about finding a summer job himself.

"Having a part-time job during term time is prohibited, but there is an exception: 'This shall not apply to helping out with a family business.' And if it's helping with a classmate's family business, if you apply, you can get permission to work just on the weekends. They consider it part of social studies."

In short, she was telling Satoru he could work in her family's orchard.

"The pay isn't much, but I'll ask them to pay you weekly, so if you start work now, you should be able to go on your trip at the beginning of August."

Satoru stood up, so excited he nearly kicked over his chair.

The crop was ready to harvest and a lot of customers were coming to pick fruit in their orchard. Sugi joined them to work there on Sundays, except during exam time. The hourly wages were even less than working in a small supermarket, but by the time the school closing ceremony was over, Satoru had been able to put away about 20,000 yen.

"What are you going to use your money for, Shu-chan?" Chikako asked.

"I haven't thought about it."

Which wasn't exactly true. "Hey, do you want to go and see a film?" he said, trying to make it sound as if he'd just come up with the idea.

"Your treat?" As he expected, she leaped at the idea.

"Okay. I mean, you did get me the job and all."

"Great! Maybe I'll sponge a meal off you as well."

Only just managing not to physically jump for joy, smiling, Sugi said, "Okay, okay."

"Great. You weren't joking, were you? Don't you dare change your mind later on!"

Chikako, totally thrilled that Sugi would be footing the bill, certainly wasn't viewing this as a date. But for now that was okay.

There was no need to rush things.

On the first day of the last week of July, Satoru failed to show up for work.

It wasn't like him—he was always so conscientious—and he hadn't even been in touch to explain his absence. Sugi wondered what was up.

Satoru turned up an hour late.

"I'm very sorry I'm late," he said, his face pale and stiff.

"If you don't feel well, you should take some time off," Chikako's father said, but Satoru insisted he was fine.

At lunchtime, Chikako's parents told the three of them to come back to the house. Satoru was looking paler than ever.

"What's wrong? Has something happened?" they asked.

But again, he obstinately insisted it was nothing, and wouldn't say any more.

Chikako, silently watching, spoke up. "Has something happened to your old cat?"

Satoru's lips tightened. He dropped his head and screwed up his eyes. Finally he allowed the tears to flow.

"He was hit by a car," he muttered, his voice broken, and then he couldn't say anything more. It seemed he'd just got the news that morning.

"You were really fond of that cat, weren't you?" Chikako said, putting her arm around his shoulders, to which Satoru murmured back, "He was family."

Why had he been forced to give him away? When Sugi had asked him earlier, he hadn't responded. If the cat had been regarded as part of the family, it was even more puzzling.

If he was this grief-stricken at the news, he shouldn't have given the cat away in the first place, thought Sugi, somewhat uncharitably. Perhaps he was a bit jealous of the other two and their shared love of cats.

"He was the cat we had back when my parents were still alive," said Satoru, which put Sugi in his place. God was punishing him, he figured, for having entertained a nasty thought about his poor friend.

"... And you hoped to be in time to see him." Chikako's kind words were so full of warmth.

Why am I such a low, mean person, when all I want is to

be the kind of man Chikako won't be ashamed of? thought Sugi.

He hadn't realized that Satoru's parents were dead.

But even if I had known, I would never have been as sympathetic as Chikako.

"What are you going to do about the job? Will you carry on?" asked Sugi.

Beside him, Chikako gave him a *Really? Now?* type of look.

"There's no point in going to Kokura now," Satoru said, and gave a faint smile.

Chikako interrupted him. "You really should go. Save up your money and go over there to say good-bye."

Satoru blinked in surprise.

"You have to mourn your cat properly, or you won't get over it. Don't just sit here fretting about being too late. Go there and mourn him. Tell him you're sorry you didn't make it in time, that you wanted to see him."

Sugi knew very well how deeply these words resonated with Satoru, because even he, who'd thought those mean things, was starting to tear up.

Satoru smiled, and decided to get back to work.

Toward the end of the summer holidays, Satoru set off on his trip.

When he came back again, he looked like he'd put the past to rest.

He'd brought back some souvenirs for Sugi and Chikako. For Sugi, some Hakata ramen he'd asked for, and for Chikako, for some reason, he brought back some blotting paper and a hand mirror he'd bought in Kyoto.

"Wow! This paper is Yojiya!"

Apparently, it was some famous cosmetics brand, and Chikako was ecstatic. A friend of hers called her over and she gave a hurried "Thank you!" and rushed off.

"So you stopped in Kyoto, too?" Sugi asked, and Satoru nodded.

"I was on an elementary-school trip to Kyoto when my parents were killed in a car accident. My mother had asked me to buy Yojiya blotting paper as a present for her. I looked all over but never managed to find it. A friend later managed to find some and bought it for me, but I never bought it myself."

"What about the hand mirror?"

"I just thought that I'd like to buy that for Chikako."

It hurt to hear all this.

Chikako should be the one to hear this. But Sugi didn't want her to.

He began to wish it had been somebody else who'd run into Satoru the day they rescued the Shih Tzu.

He didn't tell Chikako what Satoru had told him about Kyoto. He suppressed his guilty conscience by convincing himself that, if Satoru really wanted her to know, he'd tell her himself.

Now, he was constantly worried that he was losing his advantage of being Chikako's childhood friend.

She was always calling Satoru by his last name, Miyawaki, while she always called Sugi "Shu-chan."

Some time passed before he saw any significance in this.

If Chikako had known Satoru's feelings, she would, no doubt, have been drawn to him.

Unlike himself, shamefully struggling to be the kind of man Chikako could be proud of, Satoru was already there.

And there was that terrible experience he'd been through as a child.

In spite of losing his parents so young, having his precious cat taken away from him, and now not being in time to see it again, Satoru blamed no one for his troubles, didn't see any of it as unfair.

If it were him, Sugi would give himself over to the tragedy to make it work in his favor. He would make all sorts of lazy excuses, perhaps even exploit it to attract Chikako's affections.

How could Satoru be so relaxed and natural? The more Sugi got to know him, the more he felt driven into a corner. Satoru was a rival he would never be able to beat.

He started to feel the lesser man despite his privileged upbringing, and though he had more to be thankful for than Satoru, he began to feel dissatisfied with life. He started arguing with his parents over nothing, saying malicious things, sometimes reducing his mother to tears.

I have everything I need in life, so why am I such a mean, small person? Why can't I be kinder than Satoru, who has so much less?

Chikako, too, had been brought up like Sugi, never lacking a thing, yet she never felt like this when she was with Satoru. She seemed to naturally enjoy being with him. And this made Sugi feel even more cornered.

If things went on like this, he knew he was going to lose Chikako. And he had loved her for so much longer!

"I wonder if Satoru has a special girl he likes."

These words spilled out from Chikako one day when Satoru wasn't with them.

It was the final blow. Sugi felt crushed.

Later, Sugi found himself saying, "I've always loved Chikako. Ever since we were kids."

This confession was directed not at Chikako but at Satoru.

Sugi had expected that when Satoru heard this, he would put a lid on any feelings he himself might have for Chikako. He had deliberately confessed his feelings to Satoru, while pretending to seek his advice.

Satoru's eyes opened wide in surprise and, after a moment's silence, he smiled. "I get it."

You do get it, right? You, of all people, should definitely get it.

Thus Sugi neatly stopped Satoru from declaring his feelings to Chikako, and in the end Satoru stepped aside without ever saying a word about them.

In the spring of their last year in high school, Satoru changed schools. His aunt, who was his guardian, often moved around with work.

Sugi was truly sad that his friend was leaving, but all the same felt a rush of relief. At the time, he felt, *Now things will be okay.*

~

"H ow can you be such a good person when you've been so unlucky?"

Sugi was grumbling away before he realized what he was doing. It was the wine they'd opened at dinner. He had thought it was a good opportunity to treat Satoru to some local wine, so he'd bought some Ajiron red. This variety had a sweet fragrance and taste, and if you didn't watch yourself it was easy to overdo it.

Chikako was out of the room having a bath, her absence another reason Sugi had let down his guard.

Satoru smiled wryly. "I don't know if I'm a good person or not. But either way, I wasn't unlucky."

"What are you talking about? Are you denying that life's treated you unfairly, and trying to make me feel bad by not admitting it?"

"I don't know what you mean. The wine must have gone to your head. Try sobering up a bit before Chikako finishes her bath." Satoru pulled the wine bottle out of Sugi's reach.

∽

W e cats get all limp and squishy when we have catnip; for
humans, wine seems to do the trick.

Satoru would occasionally drink alcohol at home. He'd
down a few while watching one of those games with balls that
humans like—baseball or soccer—and start feeling happy,
and soon tumble sideways onto the floor.

If I inadvertently passed near him, he'd grab me and hug
me to his face, saying "Nana-*cha–n*" in a syrupy voice, and I
couldn't stand it. So I tried to keep my distance. Plus he stank
of alcohol.

There had been times when he drank away from the house
and came back smelling of liquor, but he was always in a good
mood. So I used to be convinced that when humans drank it
always made them cheerful. Like catnip for cats.

I'd never encountered someone like Sugi, who got all
gloomy and moody when he drank. When Chikako went to
have a bath, he suddenly started pouting at Satoru, almost like
he was cowering before him.

If drinking isn't fun, then why do it? I was hanging off the
top of the TV in the sitting room, eyeing the two men as they
talked, until Satoru finally removed the bottle of wine from
the table.

By the way, I became really fond of the TV there. Ours at
home was thin and flat like a board, but the one there was

more of a box, very enticing for a cat. Plus, it was faintly warm, and made my tummy feel toasty. Fantastic in the winter, I imagined.

It's really old, Momo told me. In the past, all TVs were this shape, apparently. Going from this perfect design to an impractical flat shape is, if you ask me, a step backward, technology-wise.

Momo told me that you could tell how old a cat was by whether or not they knew about these boxy TVs. In that house, Chikako gave priority to making things comfortable for cats and she dismissed the idea of getting one of the flat TVs. A splendid decision, in my opinion.

Why the glum look? If you're bored of it, then I'll have it back, Momo said to me.

She was stretching out her long limbs on a nearby sofa. She'd allowed me, the guest, to take her special seat on top of the TV.

It's not that I'm bored. It's just … I cast a glance at the worn-down Sugi.

I thought they were friends, but it doesn't look as though Sugi likes Satoru very much, Momo suggested.

That can't be true, I said.

Don't think he wants him here. And yet he went out especially yesterday to buy that wine. Said he'd like Satoru to try it.

Why flare up at Satoru like that then? Why say things

about Satoru's character, as though he's *upset* that he's such a good person?

He likes him, but he also envies him. My master wants to be like your master.

I don't get it. Satoru is Satoru, and Sugi is Sugi.

Exactly. But the master seems to feel that if he could be like Satoru, then Chikako would love him more.

Dear me, it sounds like it's a pretty big thing for him.

Chikako used to really like your master, is what I gather, Momo clarified.

This was going way back. Way before Momo was born, when these humans were young. She said she heard it from the cat who lived with them previously.

What did Satoru think? Did he like Chikako, too?

If a woman who held on to an old boxy TV for the sake of a cat was Satoru's wife, now that might be really wonderful, is what I was thinking.

Well, that's not something we know. It's just that, when it comes to Chikako, the master seems to have a guilty conscience regarding Satoru, said Momo.

Sounds like an awkward business to me. I mean, Chikako ended up choosing Sugi and became his wife, so what's the problem?

Among cats, when a female chooses a mate, it's a very clear-cut thing. Not just among cats, but with all animals, the female's judgment about love is absolute. Of course, I haven't experienced true love myself, having been looked after by Satoru since I was young. I was a little too gentle to have won the heart of a female when I was young. If I'd had a bigger face and a sterner expression, I might have. Like Yoshimine. If he were a cat, he'd definitely be a hit with the ladies.

But it makes sense now.

That mutt of a dog is Sugi's, isn't it?

Dogs the world over just aren't very level-headed about things. Their master says jump and they ask, "How high?" So perhaps Sugi's dog is trying to take the side of his gloomy master.

With cats, though, the master can throw a tantrum but cats don't necessarily jump. Cats always follow their own path.

Toramaru was still young and lacked subtlety.

In the evening, they let the dog inside the house, but led him immediately to another room. He didn't come at us barking like he did when we first met, but since he had been so terribly rude to Satoru, he and I were on high alert.

"Well, well, you seem to have had a few already."

Chikako was out of the bath.

"Are you going to bed now?" Chikako asked, as though pacifying a child, to which Sugi replied, "Nope," shaking his head like a spoiled brat.

"If you and Satoru are staying up, then I will, too."

Chikako and Satoru looked at each other with a smile. Their faces were glowing. Is a drunk really that endearing? To me, it just looks embarrassing. Crikey, I really hope I don't look like that when I sniff a bit of catnip.

After a while, Satoru said, "I'm feeling sleepy now, so I'm off to bed. Come on."

Satoru helped Sugi to his feet, but perhaps he was heavier than he expected, or his body more limp, because he began to stagger. Chikako got up quickly to help prop Sugi up.

In this way, the two of them got Sugi to bed.

❧

Not long after Satoru moved away with his aunt, Sugi started going out with Chikako.

They were both aiming to get into the same college. They talked it over and decided on a university in Tokyo. Chikako was planning to help out with the orchard business in the future, so if she didn't go to college outside the prefecture, she would end up spending her whole life within the confines of the district she grew up in. It was an entirely natural, innocent desire for a young girl to want to spend some part of her life in the big city.

They both passed the university entrance exams, and Chikako was to live with relatives in Tokyo while Sugi would stay in the dorm. It was a double room, and he was a bit concerned about whether he'd get on with his roommate, but the dorm had two points in its favor—the low rent and the convenient location.

He and his roommate arranged to meet up before the college entrance ceremony, and Sugi set off, map in hand, down the unfamiliar streets to locate his dorm.

The winding backstreets confused him and he wandered round in circles for a while, but he finally arrived, not too much later than the scheduled time.

He was filling out forms at the reception desk when it happened.

"Sugi!"

He didn't know anyone yet and turned around uncertainly. When he saw who it was, he was stunned.

"Satoru!" he said, before his brain froze. It was great to meet an old friend like this in an unfamiliar place, but at the same time the question of why Satoru was here, paired with his still-guilty conscience, began to play on his mind.

"I heard from Chikako that she was applying to this college, and I thought maybe you were, too. I see I was right."

"You heard from her? You mean, you guys met after you moved away?"

"No, not at all. She wrote to me."

This was back when high-school students didn't all have mobile phones.

"I gave you guys my new address, remember? And Chikako wrote me a letter. I never got a letter from *you*, though," Satoru said, teasingly.

"Hey, but I did call you a few times."

"Well, I guess when friends grow up, they lose touch. It's

the same with my pals from junior high, though we talk a lot on the phone. When I got that letter from Chikako, I thought, Wow, girls really are conscientious. We've written to each other a few times since."

And in one of the letters Satoru had apparently read about which college Chikako was applying to.

"Chikako never told me you were applying here, Satoru."

"That makes sense, since I never told her. I reckoned, if one of us didn't get in, it would feel kind of awkward."

Now that he understood, Sugi realized there was nothing to it. But still he had his suspicions—and that was the problem.

"Since we're both here, why don't we ask them if we can share a room?" Satoru asked. "My roommate hasn't appeared yet, and if we arrange it now it shouldn't be a problem."

Satoru had been in the dorm for a week already, and his kind nature meant he had already made a network of acquaintances, so they managed to swap roommates.

Chikako was delighted that Satoru was attending the same college, but sulked about not being told. "Why didn't you let me know?" she asked. She had been just about to write a letter to him to let him know that she and Sugi had both got into the same college.

The first semester flew by, and before they knew it the second semester had started.

"Sugi, I got a gift from one of the second years." Satoru

showed him some cans of beer, an upmarket brand that was seldom discounted.

Twenty was the legal drinking age, but for college students that was just official policy, and in the dorm drinks were circulated even between underage students. They made sure, though, that things didn't get out of hand, and were careful to avoid the eagle-eyed dorm mother whenever there was alcohol around.

"Oh, then I'll cadge some snacks to go with it."

Dorm students often got food parcels from home, and if the students shared whatever they received, they could all get some pretty nice things. Sugi had just received some juicy grapes, and, trading up, he managed to talk a student hailing from Hokkaido into letting him have some salmon fillets and sweets that were a specialty of the student's hometown.

Satoru would get merry when he drank, but he wasn't much of a drinker. Two cans of beer were all it took before his eyes grew bloodshot.

For some reason, the talk turned to an in-dorm romance. A freshman, quite a frivolous guy, had made repeated moves on an older girl in the dorm and kept getting shot down. The other guys found it funny, but also tried to cheer him up.

"How many times has he been rejected?"

"Eleven, so far."

Satoru, the informant, passed this on to Sugi, and chuckled. "It's so funny—he won't give in. He said that during the second semester he's going to hit the twenty mark."

"What for? Is he aiming to break some kind of record for being rejected? He's lost sight of the goal!"

"I know, but I kind of envy that sort of recklessness."

Satoru's red eyes sparkled.

"You know, in high school I sort of had a thing for Chikako."

The one thing Sugi had hoped never to hear.

"But since you were there, I reckoned it was hopeless. Still, even if I had been rejected, I wish I'd at least told her."

I wish I'd at least told her. If he had, then history would have been different.

Unable to keep it in, his voice cracked. "Please. Don't ever tell Chikako."

I wish I'd at least told her. History might still be different, even now.

"*Please.*"

Miserably bowing his head, Sugi thought, How shameful can I get? I know very well how miserable I look, yet I still go ahead and beg him.

Satoru seemed touched by his words, and his eyes widened a little. Just as they had when Sugi had asked for advice and shut him down. "Don't worry about it." He smiled. "You two probably have a stronger relationship than you think you do."

So Sugi was, in the end, successful in keeping Satoru quiet.

S ugi graduated from college, returned to his hometown and, after a few years, married Chikako. Satoru came to the wedding.

History wasn't going to be rewritten now—they'd come too far for that.

Still, sometimes Sugi would get a bit panicky when he thought of Satoru. Punishment, he thought, for having suppressed his friend's words all those years ago.

If he took in Satoru's cat, it would be a thorn in his side that would torment him for the rest of his life. But still.

Satoru was clearly troubled about what to do with his cat and had come to ask for his help, and since Sugi had won out with Chikako through unfair methods, he felt it was his duty to help.

It might seem weird for such a petty and cowardly guy like me to do this so late in the day, Sugi thought, but I really do like you, Satoru. You've had a much, much harder life than I have, yet you've always remained generous and kind. You blow me away.

I've always wanted to be more like you. If only I could be.

♋

The next morning, another meeting between the dog and me was arranged.

After breakfast, Chikako left the dining room to fetch him.

"Be a good boy this time, Tora," Chikako cautioned him as he stood behind the fence. Sugi, looking worried, was pacing around the dining room. Satoru looked a little worried, too. The only ones who kept their cool were Momo and yours truly.

Breakfast for me was a special tuna blend with a side of

chicken breast, so I was feeling pleasantly full. Give it your best shot, you hound.

The door to the room swung open.

The dog had planted himself in the doorway and was staring hard in my direction. He avoided Satoru's eyes.

Too damn right.

Yesterday, on several occasions, Sugi had scolded the dog, reminding him that Satoru was his good friend and that he mustn't bark at him. That being the case, there was only one other he could turn his fire on.

You want it, pal, then I'm more than ready for you.

The dog began to bark at me in such a frenzy he looked on the verge of losing it.

Ignoring the cries of the humans, I arched my back as high as it could go and made my fur stand on end. You don't fool around, do you? Momo murmured. High praise, indeed.

The dog would not stop barking. Satoru rushed over to hold me down so I wouldn't leap out at the stupid dog.

As long as you're here, the master and his wife will be thinking of Satoru! It's painful for my master if his wife remembers him!

I don't need to hear that. If it's a house with a stupid hound like you in it, then I'm calling the whole thing off on my own!

If it came to a fight, I was several leagues above this mutt.

You may talk big, but I bet you've never been in a life-and-death scrape. Bet you've never been in the kind of fight over territory where, if you lose, you'll have nothing to eat for days, have you, you spoiled, high-and-mighty hound?

I gave him an earful of the kind of spiel I'd perfected over the course of numerous scenes of carnage. The kind of rough language to which I can't subject you polite ladies and gentlemen.

Momo, surveying all this with total disinterest from her perch atop the TV, smiled. Pardon me, I told her. My one regret is besmirching the ears of a refined lady like yourself with such language.

Go home, damn you! The hound was close to tears, and still barking his head off.

A piddling three-year-old dog who's always worn a collar thinks he's going to beat me? Not in a hundred years, my friend. Momo's lived twice as long as me, and I've lived twice as long as *you*, pal.

I won't allow someone in this house who reminds the master and his wife of Satoru! Besides—

Shut it! Say any more and I'll make you regret it!

I had to admire the dog, though, since he still wouldn't shut up. He really was wound up.

Besides, your owner smells like he's not going to make it.

I told you to shut it!

"Nana!" Satoru yelled at me.

I had escaped from his grasp and swiped the dog with my claws.

Ruff! The dog's scream rang out. Three neat rows of wounds now ran down his brindled muzzle, and three lines of blood were faintly oozing out.

But still Toramaru didn't put his tail between his legs.

Several times, he looked as though he was about to lower it at least, but then he forced it up again. And growled more deeply.

"*Stop it*, Nana! You'll hurt him!"

The fight was already won, so I meekly let Satoru pick me up. "I'm so sorry." Satoru apologized over and over to Toramaru, and to Sugi and Chikako.

"It's okay. I'm just glad Nana didn't get bitten."

Chikako, turning pale, let out a sigh. Sugi gave Toramaru a good rap on the head with his fist.

"If you had really bitten Nana, he would have died, you know!"

For the first time, Toramaru let his tail sag between his legs. And he glared at me regretfully.

Okay, I understand. I won't count that among my victories.

"I'm sorry. I really appreciate you saying you'd look after Nana for me, but I'm going to take him back home." Satoru sounded quite sad about this. "It wouldn't be good for Toramaru, either, to have to live with a cat he doesn't get on with."

Satoru fetched the basket. As I stepped in obediently, I glanced back at Toramaru.

Thank you, Toramaru.

Toramaru looked a little dubious.

I came here on a trip with Satoru. Not to be left behind here in this house. I was trying to come up with a plan so we could go home together, and thanks to you it has all worked out smoothly.

Toramaru lowered his eyes and tilted his head, and Satoru and I headed toward the silver van.

They brought Toramaru out on a lead to see us off. Sugi kept a tight hold of it, wrapping it a few times around his hand.

Momo came out of her own accord to say good-bye. It's been a long time since I've seen a fight as definitive as that, she said, paying me a compliment.

"I'm so sorry it's turned out this way. I'm just glad Nana didn't get hurt."

"We really did hope to look after him."

Sugi and Chikako apologized, one after the other, but that only made Satoru uncomfortable. Which was understandable, seeing as how the only one who actually hurt anyone was, in the end, *moi*.

As usual, before Satoru got the van on the move, the old friends seemed to find it painful to say good-bye.

Even after Satoru was behind the wheel, Chikako kept saying she had forgotten to give him this or that, and handed him one present after another: her home-grown herbs, some fruit, and more fruit.

We really had better be going.

"Oh, by the way," Satoru called out of the open window.

"When I was in high school, I really liked you, Chikako. Did you know that?"

The way he said it was pretty blasé. Sugi's face stiffened. And Chikako said—*"What?"* Then she blinked like a pigeon that had just been shot by a peashooter, and gave a little laugh. "That was so long ago. Why bring it up now?"

"Yeah, I guess you're right."

The two of them chuckled. Sugi stood there, astonished, then gave a late-to-the-party laugh.

He might have been laughing, but he looked almost ready to cry.

The van had started moving down the drive when there was a shout.

"Toramaru!"

Toramaru wrenched hard, struggling to break free of the lead.

Hey, cat!

Toramaru was calling me.

You can stay! The master was laughing with the missus and Satoru, so it's all okay now for you to stay!

You idiot. I told you I had no intention of being left behind from the very start.

"Tora, can't you at least behave when we're saying good-bye!" Sugi tugged angrily at the lead.

Don't be cross with him. He was trying to stop me leaving.

But what with Tora barking his head off earlier, Sugi thought he was still angry.

"Is he upset?" asked Satoru. He looked in the rearview mirror at the receding figures. "His bark sounds different from before."

That's why I like you, Satoru. You're perceptive about things like that.

The silver van gave a little beep of its horn before turning a corner, sending dust into the air and leaving the bed and breakfast far behind.

I t would have been perfect if they could have looked after you."

There you go again, Satoru. That's just sour grapes. Mount Fuji's now well behind us.

If you intend to come and fetch me back one day, then you shouldn't leave me there in the first place.

I was standing on my hind legs and pawing the top of the backseat to see out of the rear window, and Satoru laughed. "The sea might not have been your cup of tea, but you do seem to have taken a liking to Mount Fuji."

'Cause Mount Fuji doesn't make that belly-shaking roar, and doesn't have that perpetual motion that'll swallow me up.

"I hope we can see it again together. Yeah, let's do that someday. And let's visit Sugi and Chikako again. We had such a nice view of Mount Fuji from our bedroom, and also— you liked that old picture-tube TV, too, didn't you?"

Yes, that's the ticket! That box-shaped TV was perfect. Just the right size to lie down, all toasty warm. Say, Satoru, what if we were to get a box-shaped TV like that?

"Sorry that ours is the thin type. They don't sell tube TVs anymore."

Ah, such a pity.

But that's okay. I can think of it as a special attraction for when we visit the Sugis next time.

And one other thing: the next time we visit, I bet you Toramaru will wag his tail at us.

∽

In the evening, a reservation came in at the bed and breakfast for that night.

"Maybe we should keep Toramaru tied up."

"True, he might still be worked up because of his fight with Nana."

Sugi took Toramaru outside and chained him to the kennel. Then he turned to Chikako, who had followed him.

"About what Satoru said a little while ago ..."

"What? Are you bothered by that?" Chikako asked.

Ouch. That hit home. "No, it's not that," Sugi stammered. "I was just wondering how you would have taken it if Satoru had told you he liked you when we were still in high school."

"Who knows?" Chikako said, shrugging. "Unless we could go back in time, I don't know how I would have reacted."

A spot-on answer, to which he had no reply.

"It might have been nice, though, to be a young girl wavering between the affections of two boys."

"Wavering?"

This took him by surprise and he couldn't help but ask her what she meant.

"Of course I would have wavered." Chikako laughed. "If I'd had two boys liking me at the same time, then that would definitely have piqued my interest."

Sugi felt like weeping, but managed to control himself.

I don't know which of us two she would have chosen, he thought. But at least I was included in the line-up.

And he felt his sense of inferiority and jealousy diminish a little.

The next time I see Satoru, I know I can be a much better friend.

Now that is a happy thought.

3½

Between Friends

A huge white ship was docked beside the wharf of the harbor.

The mouth at the bow was open wide and Satoru told me that we were going to drive our van right into it. It swallowed up any number of cars into its belly and yet it didn't sink. I must say, humans really do create some amazing things.

I mean, who in the world came up with the idea of floating a huge lump of iron on top of water? Must have had a couple of screws loose, whoever it was. It stands to reason that a heavy object will sink. No other animal in the world would try to defy the laws of nature, but humans are a very peculiar species.

Satoru hurried over to the ferry terminal to buy our ticket, but when he came back his face was all flushed.

"I'm afraid we've got a problem. They won't let you travel as a passenger like me, Nana."

He explained that he had written my name on the passenger form.

When the official at the reception desk found out that Nana Miyawaki (age six) was a cat, he had a good laugh, apparently. Sometimes Satoru can be spectacularly dense.

"Shall we get on board?"

A string of cars was already lined up and driving into the gaping mouth of the ferry, and I was starting to feel just a little bit anxious.

"Nana, why is your tail all puffed up like that?"

Oh, come on. If, worst-case scenario, the ship does actually sink, we'll be thrown overboard into the sea, won't we? I don't think I can imagine a fate more terrible.

I recalled the sea we'd visited when we were on our way back from Yoshimine the farmer's, and how that vast expanse of water, the weighty crash of the waves, had made me feel. The thought of being flung straight into it made even an intrepid cat like me shiver. Cats are no good at swimming and detest the water (though there are a few exceptions; some cats actually like to have a bath, but these are just instances of spontaneous feline mutation).

Even Satoru would have great trouble swimming to shore with me perched on top of his head clinging on for dear life.

Despite my misgivings, the silver van entered the belly of the beast. Walking with his suitcase in his left hand and my basket in his right seemed to wear Satoru out. Not long ago, he could have carried both easily.

Maybe I should walk on my own?

I scratched at the lock of the basket from the inside, and Satoru told me to stop. He tilted the basket so the door was facing upward. Whoa, I said, and slipped backward onto my bottom.

"Animals aren't allowed loose on the ferry, so you'll just have to be patient."

By animals, this would include dogs, too, I assumed. Fair enough. There are plenty of hotels that allow pets in general but turn away cats. They complain that cats sharpen their claws on the furniture, and so on. But for guests with cats, all they need to do is add an extra fee to cover any repairs, right?

Plus, this *animal smell* that bothers humans is much less strong in cats than it is with dogs, am I right?

Even so, this *dogs okay, cats not okay* attitude is really offensive from a feline perspective. In that sense, it's much easier to accept if neither cat nor dog is allowed. The upshot? I was liking this ferry.

Satoru took me to the pet room in the ship, where all the traveling animals were kept.

It was a spartan, neat room, and several spacious cages were stacked up to the ceiling. Today, there seemed to be a lot of passengers traveling with animals, for almost all ten of the cages were occupied. There was a white chinchilla, but that was the only other cat. The rest were a mix of dogs of varying sizes.

"This is Nana. Please be nice to him until we arrive."

Satoru went out of his way to greet the passengers already in the pet room, and put me into one of the cages.

"Will you be okay, Nana? You won't be too lonely?"

Lonely, surrounded by all these other dogs and a cat? Hardly! In fact, I'd prefer somewhere more peaceful. The dogs seemed to want to talk, and because there were so many of them, they were all yapping back and forth. And muttering complaints about me, like, *Well, look at this, will you? A mongrel cat that the human dragged in.* Well, hey, *sooorry!*

"I really wish we could have gone the whole way in the van. I'm sorry about that," Satoru said.

Not to worry. It's only for a day, so I can put up with it. Cats might not seem it, but we are nothing if not patient.

On this trip, it seems like we'll still have a long way to travel even after the ferry has docked. And Satoru gets tired easily these days.

"I'll come as often as I can to check on you, so if you get lonely, just hang in there."

Any chance you can refrain from the overprotective comments in front of the others? You're embarrassing me.

"Hello there. I hope you two cats will get on."

Satoru was peering into the cage just below mine, the one with the chinchilla in it. I was in my cage, so I couldn't see, but since the moment we arrived it had been curled up in a corner.

"This one seems lonely, too. Maybe he's feeling afraid, with all the dogs around today."

No, you guessed wrong. The curled-up chinchilla's tail had been twitching all this time, and it was obvious to me that what he was feeling was annoyance and irritation at the dogs' incessant chatter.

"Okay, I'll see you later, Nana."

His suitcase in hand, Satoru left, closing the door carefully behind him.

And the dogs immediately tried to make conversation.

So—tell me—where ya from, and where ya headed? What kind of guy is your master? In an instant, I understood exactly how the chinchilla felt, curled up there in disgust, and I copied his way of dealing with it.

I was still curled up in the back of my cage, pretending to be asleep, when the door opened wide and in stepped Satoru.

"I'm sorry, Nana. I guess you really are lonely in here."

After that, he came back to check on me another ten times. With Satoru popping in and out more often than the other owners, before long the dogs started teasing me about it. Every time Satoru left the room, there would be a noisy chorus of *Pampered! Pampered!*

Knock it off, you hounds! I growled, and was about to curl up again in the back of the cage when the chinchilla, directly below me, addressed the room.

Carrying on like a bunch of brats—you chaps are really starting to annoy me. Don't you understand? It's his *master* who's the lonely one?

For an expensive-looking long-haired breed, this cat had quite a mouth on him. The dogs all grumbled back, *Yeah, but... You see, Nana's master said Nana was lonely, didn't he?*

For dogs, you lot have a rubbish sense of smell. That master gives off a smell that says he's not going to be around for long.

So he wants to spend as much time as possible with his darling cat.

In an instant, the dogs had piped down. *It's too bad. The poor guy*, they started to mumble in hushed voices. To tell you the truth, they weren't very subtle about it. But I forgave them. They were all young dogs, and none too bright.

Thank you for that.

I aimed this at the invisible cage below me, and the chinchilla shot back with a sullen *They were getting on my nerves, that's all.*

The next time Satoru appeared, the scolded hounds all wagged their tails enthusiastically at him. "Wow," Satoru said happily, "you guys really are happy to see me, aren't you?" and he reached in through the bars of one or two of the cages to stroke the occupants. Not the sharpest pencils in the box, these dogs, but I'd have to say they were pretty docile and decent types.

After this, we cats occasionally joined in the dogs' idle chatter, and time passed by on our unremarkable sea voyage. Most of the time, though, we talked at cross purposes. We couldn't fathom, for instance, why the dogs were so into snacks like canine chewing gum and other stuff.

At midday the following day, the ferry arrived safely at its destination—the island of Hokkaido. Satoru came to fetch me first thing.

"I'm sorry, Nana. You must have been lonely."

Not at all. I had a good chat with that barbed-tongued

chinchilla. I was just thinking it would be great if I could say my good-byes to him face to face, when Satoru turned my basket around so the open door was facing the room.

"Nana, say good-bye to everyone."

See you all, I said, and the hounds' tails wagged in unison.

Guddo rakku!

This from the chinchilla, in some language I didn't understand.

Guddo ... what?

It means "good luck." My master often says it.

Come to think of it, the chinchilla's master, a foreigner with a Japanese wife, had come to see him during the journey. The cat had learned human language mainly from Japanese people, but apparently understood a lot of what his master said, too.

Thanks. *Guddo rakku* to you, too.

We bid farewell to the pet room, made our way down to the car deck and climbed into our silver van.

When we emerged from the mouth of the ferry, we were greeted by wall-to-wall blue sky.

"Hokkaido, at last, Nana."

The land was flat and sprawling. Outside the window was what looked like an ordinary city, but everything seemed much more spread out. The roads, for instance, were far wider than those around Tokyo.

We drove for a while before reaching the suburbs. There

wasn't much traffic, and we enjoyed a leisurely drive, listening to upbeat music as we went.

The road was bordered with a lovely profusion of purple and yellow wildflowers.

You could just leave the roads in Hokkaido as they were and they'd look pretty gorgeous. Not at all like the roads in Tokyo, which are surrounded by endless concrete and asphalt. Even in the more built-up areas here, the hard shoulders are all dirt. Because of that, perhaps, it's easy for the soil to breathe and the flowers to thrive. The scenery was very soothing.

"The yellow ones are called goldenrods, but I don't know about the purple ones."

The flowers had caught Satoru's eye, too. The jumble of colors was that striking. The purple wasn't one block of color but various gradations from light to dark.

"What do you say we stop for a bit?"

Satoru pulled over to the shoulder. I got out, with Satoru carrying me. An occasional car passed by, so he held me safely in his arms and wouldn't let me down as he climbed up to the purple flowers.

"They might be wild chrysanthemums. I had imagined them to be a bit neater and tidier, though ..."

The wildflowers pushing up vigorously from the soil had stems covered with blooms, like an upside-down broom. Not at all what you'd call graceful; more forceful and vigorous than that.

Oh!

As soon as I spotted it, I reached out my paw. A honeybee was buzzing among the flowers.

"Careful, Nana. You might get stung."

Hey, what are you going to do? It's instinct. I clawed at the bee and Satoru brought my paws together in his hand and held them there.

Damn it. It's exciting to play with the insects flying around. Let me go, I said, straightening my legs against his arms to get free, but Satoru held me tight and put me back in the van.

"If you just caught them, that would be fine, but I know you'll eat them, too. And we can't have you getting stung inside your mouth."

Well, you catch something, you've got to take a bite out of it. Back in Tokyo, when I killed cockroaches I'd always take a bite. The hard wings were like cellophane so I didn't eat those, but the flesh was soft and savory.

Every time Satoru found the remains of a cockroach I'd left, he'd scream. I don't understand why humans have such an aversion to them. Structurally, they're not so different from *kabutomushi* and drone beetles, the kind kids collect as pets. If it was one of those beetles, you can bet he wouldn't scream like that. But from a feline point of view, their speed makes them both challenging and fun to catch.

We continued our drive along a river, then down a hill, and emerged on a road that ran alongside the sea.

Waa—

"Wow."

We both shouted out at almost the same instant.

"It looks just like the sea."

He was talking about the pampas grass which spread out along both sides of the road. Its white ears covered the flat, sprawling fields from one end to the other, and swayed in the wind like white, cresting waves.

It hadn't been long since we last stopped, but Satoru pulled over again.

Even though there were so few cars on the road, Satoru came around to the passenger side and carried me out. He must have been afraid I might leap out. A little overprotective, I thought, but if that makes him feel better, I'm happy to let him take charge. Satoru had big hands and I felt secure and calm whenever he held me.

I wanted to see this scenery from a slightly higher vantage point, so I slipped from his hands onto his shoulder and stretched my neck. I was now just at Satoru's eye level.

The wind was rustling, the ears of the pampas grass swaying. The waves were rolling further than the eye could see.

It was just as Satoru had said. This was like a sea on land. Unlike the sea, though, there was no heavy booming sound. In this kind of sea, I might be able to swim.

From his shoulder, I leaped down to the ground and nosed my way into the pampas grass.

The path before me was blocked by the thick stems. I lifted my head and saw, far above me, the white ears waving against a clear blue sky.

"Nana?"

Satoru's worried voice reached my ears.

"Nana, where are you-uuu?"

There was the sound of dry grass being trampled so I knew that Satoru had entered the pampas grass sea, too. I'm here, just here, just near you.

But as he called me, Satoru's voice drifted further away. From where I was, I could see Satoru, but he couldn't see me, hidden as I was by the pampas.

I guess I have no choice, I thought, and followed quickly after Satoru so he wouldn't get lost.

"Nana?"

Right here! I answered him, but it seemed like my voice was being carried away by the wind and didn't reach him.

"*Naaaaana!*"

Satoru began to sound desperate.

"Nana! Nana, where are you-uuuuu?"

Satoru started to call out into the distance and, unable to bear it, I let out a loud shout, as big as I could make it.

I'm right heeeere!

And then there he was, framed against the sky, gazing down at me. The instant our eyes met, his stern look melted. His eyes softened and light caught the trails of water sliding down his cheeks.

Without a word, he knelt down on the earth, placed his big hands around my middle and hugged me. That hurts! My guts are going to squeeze out.

"You silly thing! If you wander off in here, I'll never be able to find you!"

Satoru's whole body shook with his sobs.

"For someone your size, this field is like a sea of trees!"

A "sea of trees" is how Satoru had described it to me earlier. Inside a forest like that, internal compasses don't function and you totally lose your way.

You're the silly one. I'd never wander so far that I'd actually lose you.

"Don't leave me ... Stay with me."

Ah-hah! *Finally.*

Finally, he had said what he really meant.

I'd known for a long time how Satoru felt.

I knew he was searching hard for a new owner for me, but that as each attempt came to nothing, he felt hugely relieved to be taking me home again.

"It's such a shame I can't leave him here," he'd tell each of his friends, but in the van on the way home he'd be all smiles. How could I ever leave him, having experienced that kind of love?

I will never, ever, leave him.

As Satoru wept silent tears, I licked his hand over and over, my rough tongue wandering over every knuckle and crevice.

It's okay, it's okay, it's okay. I realized how much Hachi would have regretted it—being separated from a child who loved him so much.

But Satoru was no longer a child. And I'm a former stray. So this time we should be able to make things work out.

Okay, let's get back on the road! This is our final journey.

On this last trip, let's see all sorts of wonderful things. Let's make a pledge to take in as many amazing sights as we can.

My seven-shaped crooked tail should be able to snag every single marvelous thing we pass.

Back in the van and driving off, the doves-about-to-appear CD came to an end. Then a woman's low, husky voice started to sing strangely and in a foreign-sounding language I couldn't understand.

The doves-about-to-appear song was one his mother liked, apparently, while his father preferred this one, with the husky-voiced woman singing.

The road was lined as far as the eye could see with those purple and yellow flowers.

We continued driving at a leisurely pace. Hmm ... when was the last time we had to stop at a traffic light?

We were no longer by the seaside but heading inland, and sturdy-looking wilderness spread out on either side. Finally, we could see cultivated, rolling hills.

I was in awe of this land, so flat and magnificent. It was like nothing I'd ever seen.

Wooden fences lined the roads now, and in the plots behind them there were—well, I wasn't at all sure *what* they were. Large animals, noses to the ground, chomping away at the grass. What the hell *were* those things?

I put my paws up and pressed them against the passenger

window, stretching up as far as I could. I often did that to check out the scenery outside, so Satoru had made a seat for me out of a large box with a cushion placed on top. Whenever I saw something that piqued my interest, I'd always lean forward like this.

"Ah, those are horses. This area is all pasture."

Horses? *Those things?* I'd seen them on TV, but this was my first time seeing the real thing. On TV, they looked much bigger. The horses chewing grass along the road were certainly large, but they were also relatively slender.

I craned my neck around to take a last look back at the horses as we passed, and Satoru laughed.

"If you like them that much, let's park up for a closer look next time we see some."

In the next pasture we came to, the horses were in an enclosure quite a long way from the road.

"It's a little far away," Satoru said ruefully as he got out of the van, walked around to my side and picked me up.

When he slammed the van door shut, the horses, so distant they appeared smaller than Satoru's hands, stopped chewing grass and raised their long heads to look at us.

There was a tense moment. The horses' ears pricked up as they appraised us.

"Look, they're watching us, Nana."

Not just watching, but carefully checking us out. They wanted to see if we were a danger to them. If we had been close enough for them to realize we were just a human and a cat, they would have been relieved.

Given their size, I didn't think they needed to worry. But animals have an instinct. Whatever their size, horses are grass eaters, and grass eaters have a long history of being hunted by meat eaters. This makes them timid and skittish.

On the other hand, we cats may be small, but we're hunters. And hunters are fighters. We're on our guard, too, with creatures we don't know, but when it comes to a fight we're more than willing to face up to animals much bigger than us.

That's why when dogs meddle with cats for fun, they end up whimpering, their tails between their legs. A dog ten times our size? Bring it on!

In my view, dogs have long since given up hunting. Even hunting dogs just chase their prey for the sake of their master these days, and they don't finish it off themselves. That's the crucial difference between them and us cats; even if we're just hunting a bug, we're intent on making the kill ourselves.

This point about *killing* prey is a major divide between various animals. Horses are certainly dozens of times bigger than me, but they don't scare me.

A sense of pride suddenly swelled up in me. Pride in myself as a cat who still hadn't lost his identity as a hunter.

And for me, as a hunter, I can tell you that I'm not going to back away from what lies ahead for Satoru.

The horses stared at us for a while, then concluded perhaps

that we weren't an immediate threat and returned to chomping on the grass.

"They're a bit far away, but I wonder if I could get a photo of them with my mobile phone."

Satoru took his phone out of his pocket. Most of the photos he took with it, by the by, were of me.

But I don't think you should take one of those horses, I thought.

When Satoru held the camera out toward them, the horses' heads popped up again. And their ears shot up, too.

They stood there, stock-still, gazing at us until Satoru had taken the photo.

"Yeah, they're definitely too far away."

He gave up and put the phone away. The horses continued to stare silently.

They gazed at us right up to the moment we were back in the van and the doors were shut, before finally swinging lazily back to their meal. Apologies, my friends. Sorry to bother you, I called out.

I suppose there are animals who live like this, even though they could easily kick me, and Satoru, from here to the far end of Hokkaido.

If it is their instinct that makes them that way, then I'm glad I'm a cat and have the instinct to put up a fight. I'm happy to be a high-spirited, adventurous cat that will never be intimidated by other animals, even if they're bigger than me.

I've made my point, but just to reconfirm this: meeting those horses meant a lot to me.

On the drive, I saw even more lovely scenery for the first time.

White birches with pale trunks, mountain ash with red clusters of berries like bells.

Satoru told me what everything was called. And that the mountain-ash berries are bright red. I remember some expert on TV saying once, "Cats have a hard time distinguishing the color red."

"Wow! Would you look at how red those berries are!" Satoru called out, and that's how I learned about the color *red*. It no doubt appeared differently to Satoru, but I learned how what Satoru called red appeared to me.

"The ones over there aren't so red yet."

Every time he saw trees through the window, Satoru would talk to me about them. So I became quite skilled at discriminating between different shades of red. I just learned to distinguish, in my own way of seeing things, the variations of red that Satoru pointed out, but also that they did all indeed share the same color. For the rest of my life, I would remember all the shades of red Satoru mentioned that day.

We saw fields, too, of potatoes and pumpkins being harvested, and fields where the harvest was over.

The harvested potatoes were stuffed into bags so huge they looked like they could hold several people, and the bags were then piled up in a corner of the field. Large pyramids of pump-kins were stacked up on top of the black, damp soil.

And here and there on the gentle hills were gigantic black or white plastic bundles. I was wondering why someone had left these toys behind, but they turned out to hold cut grass.

"They have a lot of snow in the winter here, so before it falls they have to harvest the grass so their cows and horses will have enough to eat."

Snow—I've seen some of that white stuff falling in Tokyo. It melted pretty swiftly, though, so it was nothing to get worked up about. That's what I was thinking at the time. But once winter arrived, I began to realize, the snow here would be a whole other story. Whenever there was a snowstorm and you couldn't see anything in front of you, even I, strong as I am, would be tossed mercilessly into the air. But that's a tale for another time.

Countryside snow that piles up to the eaves, versus city snow that melts away in a few days. It made me wonder, hon-estly, how they could both go by the same name.

As we drove on, taking the occasional break at a small supermarket, the scenery became more mountainous. Finally, the sun began to set.

We crossed a mountain pass as it did so, and another town came into view. As the silver van drove on, the sky fell darker by the moment, as if playing tag with the night.

"It's too late today. And we can't buy any flowers," murmured

Satoru, sounding put out, though still he didn't head straight for our hotel but turned off the main road.

We continued down a minor road until we reached the end of the town, where we climbed a gentle hill. At the top was a wrought-iron gate. We drove straight through it.

The land here stretched out in all directions. It was neatly partitioned into squares, and in each square was a line of square stones. I knew what they were because I'd seen them on TV.

They were graves.

Apparently, humans like to have large stones put on top of them when they are dead. I remember thinking, as I watched a program on TV about it, that it was a strange custom. The people on the program were discussing how expensive graves were, and so on.

When an animal's life is over, it rests where it falls, and it often seems to me that humans are such worriers, to think of preparing a place for people to sleep when they are dead. If you have to consider what's going to happen after you die, life becomes doubly troublesome.

Satoru drove the van through this huge area as if he knew exactly where he was heading, and at last came to a halt somewhere in the center of it all.

We got out, and Satoru walked slowly among the graves. After a while, he came to a halt in front of a grave with a whitish stone.

"This is my father and mother's grave."

It was the final spot that Satoru had been so longing to visit.

I don't get why humans like to have a huge stone put on top of them when they kick the bucket. But I do understand why they might want to look after a splendid stone like this.

I got the sense that the long drive was becoming too much for Satoru, but still, he had made it, in his silver van, with me by his side, his cat with the number-eight markings and the crooked tail like a seven.

Cats are not so heartless that they can't respect those sorts of emotions.

"I wanted to pay my respects with you here, Nana."

I know, I said, rubbing my forehead vigorously along the edge of his parents' gravestone.

It's a great honor to meet you. Hachi was a wonderful cat, I'm sure, but don't you think I'm rather nice, too?

"I'm sorry. I was in a hurry, so I'll bring flowers tomorrow," Satoru said, squatting down at the grave. There were some slightly wilted flowers in a vase.

"Ah, I see," Satoru murmured. "It was Higan recently, the time of year when people visit graves ... My aunt must have come."

Satoru tenderly stroked the wilting petals.

"I'm sorry I haven't been able to come here much. I should have visited you more often."

I stepped away from the grave, to give Satoru some time

alone. If I disappeared completely from sight, I knew he would become anxious, so I lingered where he could see me.

During the five years I'd lived with Satoru, he'd left home only a couple of times to visit this grave.

"Someday, I'll take you with me, Nana," he had said. "You look just like Hachi, and my father and mother will be so surprised.

"Someday," he had promised me, "we'll go on a long trip together." And now it was happening.

"Nana, come here!" Satoru called me and put me on his lap. As he stroked me gently, running his wide hand across my whole body over and over, I wondered what he was talking about so silently with his parents.

This town was Satoru's mother's hometown, it seemed. His grandfather and grandmother, who were farmers, had passed away fairly young, and Satoru's mother and his aunt hadn't been able to keep up the farm, so they let it go. His mother had apparently regretted this for the rest of her life.

Especially after Satoru became part of their family.

A hometown where the only thing left is a grave has to be a bit sad for a child. But there were only a few relatives on Satoru's mother's side, and they had all moved away, so what could you do?

There are so many things in life that are beyond our control.

Satoru finally straightened his legs, enveloping me tightly in his arms.

"We'll be back tomorrow," he said, then turned to the van.

We drove in silence through the now completely dark town toward our lodgings for the night.

We were staying in a cozy hotel that had a few rooms reserved for humans who had pets with them. It was a very sensible little place, I must say.

Satoru must have been exhausted from all the driving, because he went out once to get something to eat but came back within the hour and fell heavily onto the bed and into a deep sleep.

The next morning, though, he got up early.

He swiftly packed his bags, and when we emerged from the hotel the sun was still just coming up.

"Darn, the florist's isn't open yet."

Satoru made one circuit of the area in front of the station and seemed at a loss.

"Maybe somewhere will be open on the way to the cemetery ..."

He'd sort of jumped the gun starting off so early, with the flower shop still closed. On the way, he pulled up at the side of the road.

"Guess we'll have to make do with these."

And the flowers he started picking were the purple and yellow flowers that had decorated the road we had been driving on the previous day.

I liked them! They were much more beautiful than any

you'd buy in a shop, and Satoru's father and mother would be thrilled to be given them.

I searched out some wild chrysanthemums with open blooms and showed him. "So you're looking for flowers, too, eh?" He laughed and plucked the very ones I'd been rustling around in for him.

He gathered an armful and we continued on to the cemetery.

It had been dark yesterday, so I hadn't noticed, but from the top of the hill you could see the town in the distance. All the way to where the urban landscape became countryside.

The cemetery had a much more cheerful feeling in the early morning than it had the previous night, though, come to think of it, even when we'd visited in the dark yesterday, I hadn't felt at all frightened. One associates graves and temples with ghost stories, but this place had none of that gloominess, or any sense that a resentful spirit might appear at any moment.

You ask if we cats can see ghosts. Don't you know that there are things in this world that are better left a mystery?

Satoru, with flowers and garden tools (he must have bought these last night) in his arms, got out of the van.

After cleaning the gravestone, he took the wilting flowers from the vase, changed the water and replaced them with the new ones he'd just picked, their colors bright and festive.

The vase was overflowing now, and half the flowers were

left over. "I'll use these later," he said, and wrapped them in some damp newspaper and put them in the back of the van.

Satoru unwrapped the buns and cakes he'd bought and left these as offerings at the grave. Ants would no doubt soon swarm over them, and crows and weasels would come and whisk them away, but it was better than leaving them to rot.

Satoru then lit some incense at the grave. Apparently, in his family, it was the custom to light a whole bundle at once. I found it a bit too smoky, and slunk upwind to escape it.

Satoru sat down by the grave and gazed at it for a long time. Claws in and tucking my two front paws beneath my chest, I snuggled up on his knees, and he beamed at me and tickled under my chin with his fingertips.

"I'm glad I could bring you, Nana," he whispered in a small voice that was barely audible.

He sounded really happy.

I stepped away from Satoru and took a stroll nearby, staying close so he could still see me. Below the low hedge that bordered the site, stringy butterburs grew.

And below those a cricket or something was leaping around. I sniffed around in them until Satoru came over.

"What's up, Nana? You've burrowed pretty deeply into those butterburs."

Well, the thing is, underneath here is ...

"Something's in there?"

Yeah, something very nimble indeed. It was just a quick glimpse, but I saw it jump. And it left behind a strange smell.

I kept sniffing below the butterbur leaves, and Satoru laughed.

"It might be a Korobokkuru."

Come again?

"Tiny people that live under the butterbur leaves."

What? That's news to me. Are there really weird creatures like that in the world?

"They were in a picture book I loved as a child."

Ah—it's just a story.

"My parents loved that story, too. As I recall, they were both really excited when I was able to read that book by myself."

Satoru told me all kinds of things about those tiny people, but since it was all, from a feline point of view, less than enthralling, I yawned deeply, showing my pointed teeth, and Satoru smiled.

"I suppose you're not very interested."

What can I tell you? Cats are realists.

"But if you do happen to see one, don't catch it, okay?"

Okay, okay. Message received. If they really are there, I'd be itching to grab them, but out of deference to you, Satoru, I'll hold back.

Satoru sat down in front of the grave one more time. Then at last he stood up, and said, "See you later." He looked calm and refreshed, as if he had done what he had come to do.

We drove off again and before long Satoru was pulling up at another grave.

"My grandfather and grandmother."

He placed all the leftover flowers at this grave and, as before, he unwrapped some buns and cakes and left them as offerings, then burned some incense.

"All right. Let's hit the road."

The next destination was Sapporo, where his aunt lived.

The silver van was heading off on its final journey.

It happened as we were driving down a fairly nondescript stretch of road.

The road cut through a hill which sloped steeply on either side. Rows of white birches covered the embankments. From halfway down the trunks of the birches, the ground was covered with thick, striped bamboo.

In Hokkaido, this was entirely ordinary, nothing-special scenery.

We were driving along when suddenly Satoru gave a little yelp and braked to an abrupt stop. The sudden halt made me lurch forward and I pressed my claws into my cushion to steady myself.

Hey, what is going on?

"Nana, look over there!"

I turned to look out of the window in the direction of his pointing finger. And whoa, talk about surprising!

Two large deer, and a smaller one, with spots on their backs. Probably parents and child. With the pattern on their backs, they blended in with the undergrowth. Pretty darn good camouflage.

"I didn't notice them at first, but then one of them moved."

This particular deer had a puffy white heart-shaped bottom.

"Shall I roll down the window?"

Satoru leaned over to the passenger side, pushed the button and the window began to open with a mechanical whir. And with that, the deer family turned in unison in our direction.

There was tension in the air.

Ah—I get it. These animals are similar to those horses. If you were to divide animals into those two categories, they're the hunted.

"I must have put them on their guard."

Satoru stopped the window and watched their reaction. All three deer were staring at us steadily, then the two parents began to lope away up the hill.

The young deer, left behind, held our gaze, its sense of wariness still not fully developed.

His parents, apparently exasperated, seemed to call down to him from the top of the embankment, and the young deer, flashing its white heart-shaped little rear end at us, bounded up the slope.

"Ah, it's gone …"

Satoru stared regretfully after it.

"But that was amazing. I've never seen deer like that beside the road."

It's got to be thanks to my tail. Just you wait—my crooked, seven-shaped tail is bound to snag lots more wonderful things.

And the perfect example of this came not long after we had watched the deer disappear.

The scenery was, typically, nothing special for Hokkaido. Gentle hills with softly wooded areas running into one another.

Just as we were heading into a thin layer of gray cloud, it started to rain. The kind of rain you see on a sunny day, just a light scattering of drops.

"That's really something. That's the exact boundary where the rain begins."

Satoru drove on, happy, but most cats find rain very depressing. I hoped it would stop soon, and, amazingly, it did start to let up and the sun fought its way through the clouds.

In the driver's seat, Satoru gave a massive gulp. I was napping and twitched my ears at the sound. He braked gradually before pulling over to the side of the road.

In the sky above a hill before us was a vivid rainbow.

One end of the rainbow was rooted in the hill. We followed that arc with our eyes and found the other end rooted in the opposite hill.

I'd never seen the end of a rainbow in my entire life. And Satoru hadn't either, I gathered, the way he was holding his breath.

We were both seeing something extraordinary together for the first time in our lives.

"Shall we get out?"

Gingerly, Satoru got out of the car, as though he was afraid any sudden move would disturb the rainbow.

With both hands, fingers widened, he lifted me up out of the passenger seat, and the two of us gazed upward.

The rainbow's two ends were firmly anchored in the ground. The top was a little fainter, but the rainbow was entirely whole. It made a perfect arch.

I'd seen these colors somewhere before. I thought about it, and then it dawned on me.

The flowers at the graveyard that morning. The wild purple chrysanthemums, the color of each slightly different, the bright-yellow goldenrod, and the cosmos.

Cover that bouquet of flowers with some light-colored gauze and it would be just like a rainbow.

"We offered a rainbow, didn't we, at the grave?"

It made me happy when I heard Satoru say this. The two of us were on exactly the same wavelength.

Instead of getting all puffed up about it, I threw my head back and looked directly upward, and saw one more extraordinary sight.

I gave a long meow, and Satoru looked up to see what had caught my attention.

Above the perfect arc of the rainbow was another—faint, but still continuous—rainbow.

Satoru gulped again. "Isn't it amazing," he said again, this time his voice a little husky.

To think that we'd see this kind of thing at the end of our journey.

Satoru and I would remember this rainbow for the rest of our lives.

W e stood there for a long time, until the weather cleared and the rainbow evaporated into the sky.

This was our final journey.

On our last journey, let's see all kinds of amazing things. Let's spend our time taking in as many wonderful sights as we can. That's what I had pledged yesterday, when we set off.

And what incredible sights we saw.

S hortly afterward, we arrived in Sapporo, and our journey drew to an end.

4

How Noriko Learned to Love

In her previous job, Noriko had often been posted to new places, so she was used to moving. She would take what she needed out of the cardboard boxes, steadily unpacking, always in the same order. When two or three boxes had been emptied, she would flatten them to give herself more space.

She had never liked to clutter her life with household objects, so she never had many boxes to unpack.

A wall clock emerged from a box she'd just opened. The hands showed it was midday. She hadn't yet unpacked a hook to hang it on, so she placed it on the sofa in the living room. Every time she unpacked after a move, she reminded herself to pack a hook with the clock next time, but every time she forgot.

Afraid she'd lose it somewhere, whenever she moved, she'd put her phone in her pocket, and now it was vibrating. An e-mail.

It was from Satoru Miyawaki, her nephew. The child her older sister had left behind. Miyawaki had been her sister's husband's last name.

I'm Sorry, read the subject heading; it was ornamented with a cute little emoji.

I'd hoped to arrive in the early afternoon, but it looks like it'll be later. Sorry to leave you to unpack everything yourself.

He said he was going to pay a visit to his mother and father's graves. He must have lost track of time there.

She typed in a subject for her reply: *Understood.* In the body of the message she wrote: *Everything's fine here. Drive carefully.*

After she sent it, she began to feel a little anxious. Had her reply been a bit curt? It wouldn't be good for Satoru to think she'd written a cold reply because she was angry with him for arriving late.

She opened the message she'd just sent and re-read it. They were both just short messages but, compared to the warmth in his, hers came across as rather blunt. Maybe she should add something?

She typed *PS* and was going to add a new message, but nothing light and chatty came to her. Still agonizing over it, she finally typed, *Don't rush, or you'll have an accident*, and sent it. But a moment later she regretted it, just like she had the last one.

Desperate to recover from this second mistake, she sent a third e-mail. *PPS*, she typed. *I'm worried you'll be concerned about being late and drive too fast.* As soon as she sent it, she realized she'd got her priorities all wrong, since sending so many messages to him while he was driving might distract him from driving safely, the opposite of her intention.

Just then, another message came in. From Satoru. The title read *(Laughing)*. She breathed a sigh of relief.

Thank you for being so concerned. I'll take you up on your offer and take my time.

And another emoji at the end, a waving hand.

Worn out by her own indecisiveness, Noriko plonked herself down on the sofa. Her nephew was more than twenty-five years younger than she was, and how were they going to get on if she forced him to respond to each and every tiny little thing?

But it had always been this way between the two of them. Ever since her older sister and brother-in-law had died and she'd taken on the twelve-year-old boy they had left behind.

Her sister had always done her best for Noriko, and Noriko had tried to do the same for the son. But she could never shake off the feeling that all she'd ever done for him was to provide for him financially.

Her sister had been eight years older than her.

Noriko's mother had died when she was very young, so she could barely remember her, and her father had passed away when she was in her first year of high school. So, for Noriko, her sister had been her sole guardian.

When her father died, Noriko had said she wouldn't go on to college, but her sister had insisted that she did, arguing that it was a waste if she didn't, as she was so bright. After her older sister graduated from high school, she had worked at the local farmer's co-op, and it seemed she had given a lot of thought to the question of whether Noriko should go to college. Even if their father had still been alive, the family's financial situation would have made it difficult for both girls to go.

In the spring, when Noriko passed the exam to go and study law, the specialism she had chosen herself, straight after high school, her sister had been transferred from their hometown to Sapporo. Noriko's college was outside Hokkaido, so this meant that both of them were leaving their hometown. Her older sister had used this opportunity to sell off every piece of farmland and the woodlands her father had owned.

Selling it off piece by piece, her sister had explained, wouldn't bring in much money. Up until then, they'd been renting the land out to a neighboring farmer, but the income was minimal. Selling it all as one lot would bring in a fair amount of money, enough to cover Noriko's tuition fees and living expenses.

At first, they had been reluctant to sell the house they'd grown up in, and had rented it out, but by the time Noriko graduated from college her older sister had let this go as well. Her sister had married and the sale would raise money for Noriko's remaining tuition fees. It wouldn't do for her sister's new family to have to continue supporting her.

Her sister always used to apologize for not having waited to get married until after Noriko had graduated. But Noriko knew how patiently her new brother-in-law had waited to marry her sister. He'd been transferred away from Hokkaido in his job and had proposed to her before he was due to leave.

That was the official reason, but there was another reason her sister couldn't reveal. The young man's family was opposed to him marrying this woman who not only had no parents but was supporting her younger sister. His family were well off, and knowing her older sister was struggling financially, they had decided she was after their money.

They'd set up any number of *omiai*, arranged meetings with other women, trying to get their son to leave her, and truth be told, it had been hard for both of them to resist the pressure.

Noriko was glad her brother-in-law was not the kind of man to buckle under pressure from his family and leave her sister. She was grateful to him for this, and it never crossed her mind to oppose her sister's marriage.

"But, sis," she argued, "can't we at least keep the old house?"

"No one wants to rent it anymore. And it's getting really run-down. The person we're renting to now said if we sell it to him he'll renovate it, but otherwise they'll move out."

"That's not a bad offer ..."

"Both of us live outside Hokkaido and we can't afford the upkeep of an empty house. If we pay for the renovations, we might be able to find a new person to rent it, but financially it'll be tough. And an empty house wouldn't survive the winter snows."

Her sister had never explained the situation to her before, and for the first time Noriko had understood that she had always done her best to provide her with everything she needed.

She had hoped one day to repay her sister for all she'd done for her. But well before she could, her sister and her brother-in-law were gone forever.

At the very least, she wanted to do her best for the son they'd left behind, Satoru. That was what she had hoped, but, from the very start, she didn't feel she had managed to keep that particular ball in the air.

And it would all end with her never having done enough for Satoru either.

Sis, I am so very, very sorry.

I don't think I ever made Satoru happy.

All I do is make him worry over trivial things like this. The e-mail with the title *(Laughing)*. He joked around, but you could sense the tender concern that was so typical of Satoru.

Ever since she had started looking after him, Satoru had been a reasonable, very perceptive, mature child. But was this really his true nature?

Her sister had always insisted he was a mischievous boy who gave her a lot of trouble, though she'd always smiled when she said this.

And it was true that, while his parents were still alive, Satoru had been pretty naughty. When Noriko went on the occasional visit, she had found him big-hearted and self-assured, as children who know how fiercely they are loved often are. "Auntie, Auntie," he'd say, clinging to her, and sometimes he'd throw a tantrum or sulk.

A typical child, in other words, yet when he came to live with her he never once acted selfishly. This seemed less because his parents' death had forced him to mature quickly than because Noriko had compelled him to be that way.

She had no idea how to overcome the distance she'd created between herself and the young Satoru, and she generally relied on him to paper over her sense of estrangement.

I hope he can at least spend these last days free of worry. She truly felt that way, and yet she couldn't even do a decent job of exchanging a few e-mails with her nephew.

At least, Noriko thought, as she got up from her short rest on the sofa, *at least I can get everything in order here before Satoru arrives.* She might be lousy at sorting out the subtleties of other people's feelings, but even an obstinate, unsociable person like her could buckle down and get the job done when she had to.

It was nearly three o'clock when Satoru finally drove up to the apartment.

"Sorry, Aunt Noriko, for being so late."

"Don't worry. I get things done faster by myself."

She'd meant to respond lightly to his apology, but Satoru looked a little embarrassed. Seeing his expression, she realized that, yet again, she'd said the wrong thing.

"I have no problem at all with us living together. I'm your legal guardian, after all." She'd hurriedly added this, but again it was something that would have been better left unsaid. The more she tried to explain herself, the faster her speech became.

"The only things left unpacked are yours, Satoru. I put the boxes in your room. I've pretty much finished putting everything else away, so you don't need to help with that."

When she saw Satoru's face, as he looked at her, blinking in surprise, she realized she'd been firing off one comment after another without giving him a chance to respond.

"I'm sorry. I'm afraid I'm the same as ever . . ."

Her shoulders slumped dejectedly, and Satoru suddenly let out a small laugh.

"I'm *glad* you haven't changed, Aunt Noriko. We haven't lived together for thirteen years and, to be honest, I've been feeling a bit nervous about it."

Satoru then put the bag he had slung across his shoulder on the floor, and with both hands placed the basket carefully beside it.

"Nana, this is your new home."

He opened the basket door and a cat leaped right out. The cat had markings shaped like the character for eight on his forehead, and a black hooked tail. Other than that, it was pure white. She had the feeling that the cat Satoru had had years ago, the one they'd had to give away when she took her nephew in, had looked similar.

The cat had its nose to the ground, sniffing tentatively.

"I'm sorry that taking me has meant taking in Nana as well." Satoru frowned. "I was hoping to find a place for him before we started living together, but I just couldn't find a decent new owner. Though a number of people did offer."

"It's quite all right."

"But it's meant you've had to move into a new apartment."

He'd told her he would find someone to take Nana before he moved out of his place in Tokyo, but that hadn't worked out, so here he was, cat in tow. Noriko had moved out of the apartment she was in, which forbade pets, and had found a new place that allowed them.

This new apartment was also in a good location, convenient for Satoru's visits to the hospital.

"Ah, I see you found something nice, Nana."

Satoru narrowed his eyes as he looked at the cat. Noriko looked over, too, and saw that the cat was sniffing around one of the cardboard boxes that had yet to be flattened.

"Why does he like that box, I wonder?" To Noriko, it was just a cardboard box.

"Cats like empty boxes and paper bags. And narrow spaces, too."

Satoru squatted down next to the cat, and Noriko noticed how thin his neck was, like an old man's, far too small for the collar of his shirt.

And he's still so young.

Noriko felt a sharp pain deep in her nose and hurried off to the kitchen.

As she was more than twenty-five years older than Satoru, she felt it would have made more sense if she'd gone first.

I'm really sorry, Aunt Noriko."
    She recalled the day of that desperate phone call. A test had revealed a malignant tumor. He needed an operation immediately.

She'd traveled to Tokyo first thing. The doctor wasn't optimistic, and with each word he spoke, it felt as if all hope was fading.

Best to operate right away, she was told, and though they did, the operation turned out to be ineffective. Tumors had spread throughout his body and all they could do was close up the areas they'd cut open.

One year left to live.

After the surgery, Satoru had lain in the hospital ward, smiling with embarrassment.

"I'm sorry, Aunt Noriko."

There he goes again.

She half told him off for apologizing. Satoru said he was sorry again, and was about to apologize for saying sorry, but swallowed back the words.

Satoru decided to leave his job, move from Tokyo and live with Noriko. When he finally had to be hospitalized, Noriko would go to the hospital to look after him.

Noriko worked as a judge in Sapporo but had stepped

down from her job in order to be with Satoru. Judges are constantly being transferred and, if she hadn't stepped down, there was no guarantee that she wouldn't be transferred just as Satoru was breathing his last. Taking advantage of her connections, she found a job as a lawyer in a law firm in Sapporo.

Satoru worried about Noriko having to change jobs, but she had been thinking all along of working as a lawyer after the mandatory retirement age for a judge. This just speeded things up a bit.

In fact, she regretted not having thought about changing jobs long ago, when she had first started looking after Satoru.

If she was able to leave her position as a judge now, she could have done so back then. Back when Satoru was at an impressionable age, she'd forced him to transfer to a new school repeatedly, yanking him away from friends and places he'd grown comfortable in.

If he's going to leave this world at such a young age, she thought, the least I could have done was to give him a happier childhood.

Holding back the tears, she pretended to be straightening things up in the kitchen. Just then, Satoru called out to her from the other room.

"Aunt Noriko, is it okay if we leave one small cardboard box and don't flatten it? Nana really seems to like it."

"When he gets tired of it, be sure to put it away."

She said this intentionally loudly so he wouldn't notice the tears in her voice.

"Did you find the parking spot okay?" she went on.

She'd rented one space in the basement parking area for Satoru to park his van.

"I did. Number seven, on the corner. Did you pick number seven especially for me?"

Satoru seemed so pleased it was the same number as his cat's name.

"Not really. I thought the corner spot would be easy to find, that's all."

Then she went ahead and asked a silly question.

"So Nana's name comes from *nana*—seven?"

"That's right. His tail is hooked like the number seven."

Satoru went to pick Nana up and show him to his aunt, but the cat was nowhere to be seen. "Nana?" he called, puzzled.

"EEEEEK!" This shriek emanated from Noriko. Something soft was rubbing against her calf.

She dropped the pan she was holding and it clattered loudly to the floor. She shrieked again as something small and furry scampered away.

Satoru scooped up the cat and burst out laughing. It seemed Noriko's shriek wasn't totally unexpected.

He spluttered painfully, he was laughing so much.

"You don't much like cats, but now you've got one in your own home."

"It's not that I dislike them, I just don't know how to handle them," she protested. Once, when she was little, she'd gone to stroke a stray cat and had been badly bitten. Her right hand—the one she had thoughtlessly touched the cat with—had swelled up to twice its usual size, and ever since then cats had been on her list of things she couldn't handle.

A sudden thought occurred to her. At what point had Satoru found out about her aversion to cats?

"But please understand that it wasn't because of my issues with cats that I didn't let you keep that cat all that time ago."

"I know. I understand."

When she'd taken Satoru in, they had to give up the cat because her job meant she was transferred so often. Most of the housing they lived in was provided by the government and didn't allow pets.

But if she had liked cats, would she have kept it? If she herself had been fond of animals—not just cats—would she have better understood the feelings of a child who had to be separated from his beloved pet?

When Satoru was on a junior-high-school trip to Fukuoka, he'd snuck out of the hotel one night. The teachers had caught him at the station, he was given a strict reprimand and his guardian was contacted, and when this happened Noriko had been shocked.

Had he been trying to visit the cat he'd had to give away? The distant relatives who had taken in the cat lived in Kokura, one stop away from Hakata on the Shinkansen train. Once Satoru had meekly mentioned wanting to see the cat, but she'd told him it was out of the question since she was too busy. As far as Noriko was concerned, the matter of the cat was settled. Now that they had someone they could trust to care for it, there was no need to travel so far just to see it.

Noriko felt a sudden rush of regret.

"I'm really sorry I didn't understand back then how much you loved that cat, Satoru. I should have taken the cat in like this for you when you were a child."

"Hachi was well taken care of until the very end, and that's good enough. Because you found decent people to take care of him."

Satoru stroked Nana, who was curled up on his lap, gently stroking each paw with the tips of his fingers and circling the central spot on his head.

"But Nana wrecked all the relationships at every home I was trying to make for him. You've really helped us by letting me bring him with me now."

Satoru held Nana's head in two gentle hands and pointed his face toward Noriko.

"Nana, you get on nicely with Aunt Noriko now, okay?"

∽

You can tell me to get on with her, but I'm still feeling a bit cross.

The reason is, Noriko is kind of rude. I'm going to live here with Satoru, and I just thought we should get on, so all I did was go ahead and say hello.

Rubbing yourself against someone's legs is the best a cat can do when it comes to a warm greeting, so what was with the big squeal, that "EEEEEK!"? It gave me the fright of my life! Sounded like she'd run into a ghost on a dark night.

Well, she *is* taking in both Satoru and me, so I suppose I can overlook it.

Our first meeting was a disaster, but our new life with Noriko began nonetheless.

Noriko was the type of person who had no clue at all about cats, and it took us a while to find the appropriate distance to keep from each other.

"Good morning, Nana."

In her own way, she tried to get used to me, and she started timidly reaching out a hand to me as she said hello. But what was she thinking, suddenly touching my tail like that? I mean, unless you're a special pal of mine, I'm not about to let anyone touch my tail. Normally, I'd give them a good whack—claws in, obviously—if they tried, but out of respect to the head of the household I confined myself to scowling and lowering my tail out of the way.

I hoped Noriko would get the message, but every time she reached out to touch me she inevitably zoomed in on my tail.

One particular morning, Satoru happened to see this and came to my rescue.

"You can't do that, Aunt Noriko, touching his tail all of a sudden like that. Nana hates it."

"Then where should I touch him?"

"Start with his head, or behind his ears. When he gets used to you doing that, then you can do under his chin."

A toothbrush in his other hand, Satoru demonstrated, stroking each area in turn around my head.

"The head, behind the ears, under the chin …"

You won't believe this, but as Noriko repeated these instructions, she took notes!

"Do you really need to take notes?" Satoru laughed.

Noriko was deadly serious. "I don't want to forget," she replied.

"Instead of notes, it would be better to practice by stroking him."

"B-but it's near his mouth."

So what if it's near my mouth?

"What if he bites me?"

The impertinence! You have the nerve to speak to me like that? A gentleman who, in spite of you suddenly touching his tail, refrained from swatting you? And you aimed for my tail more than just a couple of times!

What you said just now, now *that* deserves a bite.

"It's okay. Try it."

At Satoru's urging, Noriko very timidly reached out a hand. If that didn't deserve a bite, I didn't know what did.

However, I'm a grown-up cat and I restrained myself, so, everyone, feel free to shower me with praise.

Still, I now understood why she always went for my tail. To Noriko's way of thinking, it was the furthest point from my mouth. Though, in actual fact, all animals will react more quickly if you touch their tails or back rather than hold your hand out right in front of them.

"He's so soft."

I'd always prided myself on having fur as soft as velvet.

"See? He likes it."

To be honest, Noriko's touch was awkward and not all that pleasant, but to help train her I was quite willing to pretend that it was. Plus, I certainly didn't want her targeting my tail each and every time.

"Eeek!"

Noriko screeched and pulled back her hand. I shrank back, too. What on earth?

"His throat! The bone in his throat is going up and down. Yuck!"

This is impertinence squared! The way you touch me doesn't even feel that good. I'm only purring to make you feel better about it!

"Not to worry," Satoru explained. "When he feels good, he purrs."

As a rule, that is. This is an exception. I'm forcing myself here to give you a treat, so don't you forget it.

"But it's coming from all the way down his throat," Noriko said.

Noriko rubbed my throat with the side of her finger.

"Where did you think it would come from, if not the throat?"

"I thought it came from the mouth," she replied.

Purring from my *mouth*? What are you, an imbecile?! Excuse me—the shock has made my language deteriorate. A thousand pardons.

Noriko stopped stroking me, so I stopped purring and popped into the cardboard box that had been placed specially for me in a corner of the living room.

This cardboard box that Satoru had left out for me fitted nice and tight and was really quite cozy.

"Satoru, how long do we have to keep that box there?"

"Nana likes it, so leave it there for a while."

"But I don't like it; it feels like we're not totally unpacked. I mean, I bought him a nice cat bed and a scratching post."

A box is totally different from a bed and a post, I'll have you know.

In this way, Noriko grew used to the presence of a cat in her house.

"How's this, then?"

Noriko said this the other day while bringing in what I took to be a replacement for the cardboard box, which by now was looking pretty shabby, what with me sharpening my claws on it.

She'd taken another cardboard box, opened it up and made it wider and shallower, then reinforced it with tape.

"This one is newer and wider," she said. "I've made it with two layers of cardboard so it'll last longer when he sharpens his claws on it. So what do you say to getting rid of that tattered old box? The corners are all bent out of shape where Nana's been sleeping."

"Hmmm … I'm not sure." Satoru shot me a glance. What do you think?

I yawned back. Sorry. Zero interest. Noriko just doesn't get it. A wide box spoils all the fun; it offers none of the charms of being inside a box.

Ignoring Noriko's creation, I slipped inside the old box, and Noriko looked deflated. Satoru laughed. "Maybe it was better not to alter the box. Next time we get a cardboard box, how about just leaving it as it is?"

"But I did all that work on it."

A waste of time. Cats the world over prefer to discover things they like on their own and rarely go for anything that's been provided for them.

For a while after this, Noriko's box sat there forlornly beside the old box, but before long it was put out with the recycling.

Satoru began to visit the hospital nearly every day. It was nearby, within walking distance, but he'd go there first thing in the morning and often not get back home until evening. Maybe there was lots of waiting in line, or the tests and treatment took a long time.

Satoru had lots of marks from all the injections on his right arm, bluish-black bruises that didn't fade, and soon his left arm was the same. I only get one vaccination shot a year, and I hate it, so I was amazed that Satoru could put up with getting a million of them.

And yet, no matter how often he went to the hospital, his smell didn't get any better. As several dogs and cats had told me earlier, that *doesn't smell like he's got much longer* scent was only getting stronger.

No creatures ever get better once they have that smell.

Sometimes, Noriko cried in secret, weeping gently beside the kitchen sink or in the bathroom. The only one who knew about it was me. She forced herself never to cry in front of Satoru, but she didn't think to include a cat in the equation.

When I rubbed against her legs after that, she didn't scream anymore. And I was beginning to feel her appreciation when she fondled the back of my neck.

The town was completely white with snow, the mountain ashes that lined the streets even redder as they endured the freezing cold.

"Nana, let's go for a walk."

Satoru's strength had faded, so much so that on the days when he went to the hospital he'd sleep for the rest of the day, but still he never missed out on our walks together.

It was freezing and slippery, but except for when he was at

the hospital longer than usual or when there was a snowstorm, we went for a walk every day.

"You've never been through a winter in a place with so much snow, have you, Nana?"

The street was icy and the pads of my feet skidded on it. Icicles hung from the eaves of the buildings. The snow pushed up by the snowplows looked like mille-feuille pastry piled up along the streets.

Sparrows huddled in rows on the power lines. Dogs cheerfully plowed their way through snow banks in the park. Cats in the town quietly slipped into the few spots that would keep them out of the cold: sheds, garages, warm kitchens.

There were still a lot of things the two of us had never seen before.

"My, what a cute cat. Out for a walk?"

It was a bright, clear day, and a charming old lady at the park had called out to us.

"What's his name?"

"He's called Nana. After the shape of his tail, like a seven."

Satoru hadn't changed. He was still the same cat-loving guy, intent on explaining the origins of my name to every passerby.

"He's very well behaved, isn't he, walking beside you like that?" said the old lady.

"He certainly is."

After we'd said good-bye, Satoru picked me up, his fingers, no longer strong and broad but thinning and fragile, finding their way around my belly.

"You are very well behaved, so I know you'll be a good boy from now on."

From now on? When *hadn't* I been a good boy? Kind of impolite to have to make sure of that now, don't you think?

The streets were filled with festive lights, and, as if that weren't enough, Christmas adverts spilled out of TVs everywhere. In the evening, Satoru and Noriko ate Christmas cake, and they gave me some tuna sashimi, to which I was more than a little partial. The next morning, all their energy turned to preparing for New Year.

On New Year's Day, they gave me some chicken breast, but after sniffing it a few times I kicked sand on top of it. There was no actual sand there, of course, so it was only air sand.

"What's wrong, Nana? Don't you like it?"

Satoru looked puzzled. I would have loved to have eaten it, but it smelled funny.

"Aunt Noriko, is this chicken the same kind you always give him?"

"Well, given the occasion, I splashed out. I steamed some special local free-range chicken."

"Did you add something to it when you steamed it?"

"I poured in a bit of sake so it wouldn't smell so much."

Humph. I rest my case, Noriko.

"Sorry, but it seems like Nana can't eat it because it smells like sake now."

"Really? It was only a couple of drops."

"Cats have an excellent sense of smell."

"I thought that was dogs? Six thousand times more sensitive than humans, they say."

Noriko's not a bad sort, but at times like this she tends to overthink things. It's true that dogs are known for their great sense of smell, but that doesn't mean cats don't have a good nose. I mean, no one needs a sense of smell six thousand times better than humans to discern that sake has been sprinkled on a chicken breast.

"Cats are way more sensitive to smell than humans as well."

Satoru was in the kitchen, and he prepared my usual safe, high-quality chicken breast and brought it over to me on a clean plate, taking away the chicken that had had those unnecessary things done to it.

"That sake-steamed meat, I'll put it in my *ozoni*."

Noriko let out a deep sigh.

"Until Nana came here, I never would have imagined that a person would eat a cat's leftovers."

"It happens sometimes when you have a cat. And these aren't leftovers. He didn't touch it, so it's perfectly safe."

Satoru put the meat in his bowl of *ozoni* soup as a topping.

"What will people think if they hear I gave you something to eat that even a cat wouldn't touch? Please don't mention it to anyone."

"Anybody who has a cat will understand."

Satoru and Noriko then said "Happy New Year" to each other and started eating their *ozoni*.

"Nana's only been here three months, but in that time I've found that cats really are odd creatures."

Ah, so *that's* how you think of me, and we're barely into the New Year? I'll have you know, that's the kind of rudeness I simply can't overlook.

"And that box . . ."

The cardboard box was still in the corner of the living room. Noriko had resentfully let it be known that she wanted to toss it out before the New Year.

"A new one would be so much better . . ."

Sorry to tell you this, but you're missing the point.

"And why does he go into a box that's clearly too small for him? It's obvious it's not big enough."

Hit a sore spot, why don't you?

"The other day he thrust his front paw into a jewelry case."

"Yep, that's the way cats are." Satoru nodded happily.

"And once he tried putting his paw in a tiny box that had contained a watch."

What can I say? It's instinct, pure and simple. Cats are always looking for a nice cozy space that will fit just right.

So when I spy a nice square box that's slightly open, instinct doesn't allow me to let it go. Because maybe—just *maybe*—if I stick my paw inside, some device in there might make it expand? 'Course, up till now, I haven't had any luck at all with that.

Though I do hear there's a cat in some cold foreign country

who keeps on opening doors, thinking that, eventually, one of them will lead to summer.

"I'm sorry, but I can't eat any more."

Satoru laid his chopsticks down. For a moment, I saw a sad look cross Noriko's face. She had only put one *omochi* in Satoru's bowl. And he had barely touched the lavish spread of New Year's delicacies she'd bought specially at a department store.

"It was delicious. My mom always used to include taro root, snow peas and carrots in her *ozoni*. And the way you season it is like the way Mom did it, too."

"That's because, for me, my sister's cooking was the taste of home."

"I remember when I first came to live with you, how relieved I was to find that the food tasted like Mom's cooking. I think that's why I got used to living with you so quickly." Satoru smiled broadly. "I'm glad you're the one who looked after me."

Noriko gasped, as if surprised, and avoided his eyes. She looked down and murmured, "I ... I wasn't such a good guardian. If you had gone to live with someone else, maybe it would have been bet—"

"I'm *glad* you're the one who took me in," said Satoru, ignoring her words.

Noriko gulped again, her throat pulsing like a frog's. Now who was it, when they first met me, who freaked out about *my* throat making a funny sound? *Hm?* That's a pretty funny sound you're making yourself, if you don't mind me saying.

"But that thing I said to you, when I first took you in."

"I was going to find out someday. You didn't do anything wrong."

"But ..." Noriko sniffled as she continued to look down. Still gulping over and over like a frog, and in between gulps murmuring, "I'm sorry, I'm sorry," over and over.

"I shouldn't have said that to you."

Her voice had become husky.

❧

When Noriko heard the news of her sister and brother-in-law's deaths, she went to the funeral intent on taking Satoru in, even though she was single. Satoru was the one thing her sister would have been worried about and Noriko was determined to do whatever she could for him.

Relatives from her brother-in-law's side of the family made a token appearance at the funeral and left without touching on the issue of what was to be done with Satoru at all.

And on her side of the family there was no one else willing to make the decision to have him. When Noriko said she would, some of them were worried, saying a woman on her own might not be able to manage. Most of them suggested putting the boy in foster care.

Satoru was her sister's and brother-in-law's child. If he had no relatives, that would be one thing, but since there was a relative who had the financial resources to take him in, she would be shirking her duty if she put him into foster care, so she insisted, in spite of the resistance.

The funeral ended, the estate was settled and, soon afterward, Noriko adopted Satoru. She told him:

"You're going to find out eventually, so I'm going to go ahead and tell you now. Satoru, you are not related by blood to your father or your mother."

Reality is reality. That was her way of thinking, but when she saw the look on Satoru's face when she told him, she realized she'd made a big mistake.

Satoru grew pale, and his face contorted in shock.

It was the same blank look he had had after his parents' deaths. As he approached the two coffins set up in the local community center, he'd looked as if he had lost everything he had in the world.

Even a tactless person like her knew instantly that in a matter of seconds, because of her, Satoru had lost everything all over again.

When his friends came for the wake, he cried for the first time. Afterward, the expression on his face slowly returned to normal.

The realization that she had done something unspeakable upset her terribly.

"Then who are my real father and mother?" Satoru asked.

"Your real mother and father are indeed my sister and her husband. The others are just your birth parents."

Obviously, Satoru had done nothing wrong, but still she spoke like this, as if scolding him. She was so confused, she couldn't control herself.

"Your real parents are my sister and her husband; your birth parents merely gave birth to you. They were utterly irresponsible and they were going to let you die when you were a baby."

This had been Noriko's first big case as a judge. The couple had been quite young. It was more than a criminal case of child abandonment; it was so extreme that the birth parents had been charged with attempted murder. They'd stopped feeding the baby until he was no longer able even to cry, then had wrapped him in a black plastic bag and thrown him out on the day the rubbish was due to be collected. A neighbor had grown suspicious when he spotted the plastic bag moving and ripped it open. The couple had been walking away when the neighbor reported them.

The trial ended, and Satoru's birth parents were given the prison terms they deserved, but there was nowhere to place Satoru. The only option left was an orphanage.

The whole case had almost been too much for Noriko. Imposing a punishment that befitted the crime—that she could do, but it did nothing to secure a future for the innocent baby.

Her sister had been the one who helped her cope with this

ordeal. It was a major case, and her sister had been following it since the start.

"People should really go through a vetting process in order to get married," Noriko had grumbled at the time. "If couples with kids were all like you and your husband, sis, then this type of crime would never happen."

Just as she said this, she felt a cold trickle of sweat run down her back. After her sister had got married, she'd found out she wasn't able to have children. The criticism from her husband's family had been hurtful, and her husband had distanced himself from them, yet even so her sister remained anxious.

It was soon after this that Noriko's sister told her that she wanted to adopt Satoru. Just before he was due to be sent to an orphanage.

"It's because you told me we would be good parents," she had said, smiling.

Satoru had been devastated by the news.

"Your birth parents just gave birth to you, that's all," Noriko had reassured him. "Your real parents were my sister and brother-in-law. So it was my duty to take you in."

Noriko had said this to put Satoru's mind at ease, but she had instantly regretted using the word "duty." It sounded so stiff and formal.

"Satoru, you don't need to worry about a thing," she had added, in an attempt to make up for it.

The criticism her male relatives had of Noriko—that she needed to be more careful about what she said—was spot-on. From the very beginning, she'd got it all wrong with Satoru, telling him things she never should have.

"That's why she can't find a husband," they had said. And, she thought now, they were probably quite right. At the time, she'd had a boyfriend, but soon after she adopted Satoru they split up. Her boyfriend seemed upset that she hadn't consulted him before making the decision.

"Why didn't you talk to me about this?" he had reproached her, and she had explained that, since Satoru was her nephew, she hadn't thought she needed to.

At that moment, the barriers had gone up, and she knew it. It seemed that, once again, she'd been incredibly insensitive.

Learning to have some insight into other people's sensitivities was, she concluded, more difficult than mastering the law.

The cat that Satoru had owned ended up being taken in by a distant relative.

This relative—such a distant relation that Noriko didn't feel at all close to him—had tousled Satoru's hair and said, "Don't worry. Everyone in our family loves cats, so we'll take good care of him."

Satoru had given him a cheerful look and nodded. Not once since the day his parents died had Satoru looked at her in that way.

Occasionally, this relative would send them a photo of the

cat. But before long, these letters became few and far between, though the annual New Year's card from them always had a photo of Hachi printed on it and a short message: *Hachi's doing well!*

The family were considerate enough to let them know when Hachi died, and when Satoru went to visit the grave they welcomed him warmly.

Maybe Satoru would have been happier if they had taken him in, too—even now, the thought occurred to her sometimes. When all the other relatives had hesitated to take in this child to whom they had no blood ties, this family had said, "If only we had the means, we'd have liked to help out." They had other children already, quite a lot in those days. "It's a question of money, you know," they'd said, smiling awkwardly.

But couldn't they have taken Satoru, if Noriko had helped them out financially? Was taking him in herself just egotistical, all about her not wanting to give up the one thing her sister had left behind?

She had thought about all these things for the longest time.

Noriko had started to weep.

"I think you would have been much happier if your relative in Kokura had adopted you."

"Why?" Satoru blinked in surprise. "He's a nice man and everything, but I'm glad you took me in, Aunt Noriko."

Now it was her turn to ask why.

"Well, you're my mother's younger sister. You're the one who can tell me the most about my parents."

"But right after they died, I went and told you that awful thing—"

Satoru cut her off. "I *was* pretty shocked when I heard that, I grant you. But because you told me that, I was able to appreciate just how happy I'd been with them."

Noriko looked dubious. Satoru laughed.

"I never, ever thought they weren't my real parents. That's how much they treated me like their own child. Though my birth parents didn't want me, another man and woman loved me that much—I mean, you don't find such incredible love very often."

That's why I'm so happy. Satoru had said this to me, his face beaming, many times.

∽

I get it. Having had Satoru take me in as his cat, I think I felt as lucky as he did.

Strays, by definition, have been abandoned or left behind, but Satoru rescued me when I broke my leg.

He made me the happiest cat on earth.

I'll always remember those five years we had together. And I'll forever go by the name Nana, the name that—let's face it—is pretty unusual for a male cat.

The town where Satoru grew up, too, I would remember that.

And the green seedlings swaying in the fields.

The sea, with its frighteningly loud roar.

Mount Fuji, looming over us.

How cozy it felt on top of that boxy TV.

That wonderful lady cat, Momo.

That nervy but earnest hound, Toramaru.

That huge white ferry, which swallowed up cars into its stomach.

The dogs in the pet holding area, wagging their tails at Satoru.

That foul-mouthed chinchilla telling me *Guddo rakku!*

The land in Hokkaido stretching out forever.

Those vibrant purple and yellow flowers by the side of the road.

The field of pampas grass like an ocean.

The horses chomping on grass.

The bright-red berries on the mountain-ash trees.

The shades of red on the mountain ash that Satoru taught me.

The stands of slender white birch.

The graveyard, with its wide-open vista.

The bouquet of flowers in rainbow colors.

The white heart-shaped bottom of the deer.

That huge, huge, huge double rainbow growing out of the ground.

I would remember these for the rest of my life.

And Kosuke, and Yoshimine, and Sugi and Chikako. And above all, the one who brought up Satoru and made it possible for us to meet—Noriko.

Could anyone be happier than this?

I t must have made you sad that we had to move all the time because of my work. Every time you made friends, I had to tear you away."

"But I made new friends wherever we went. I was sad to say good-bye to Kosuke, but in junior high I met Yoshimine, and in high school I met Sugi and Chikako. Our *omiai* meetings didn't go so well with any of them, but they all said they'd take Nana for me. I've been so lucky to have this many people willing to take care of my darling cat."

Satoru reached out his thin hand and covered Noriko's fingers.

"None of the people who offered to take Nana were right for him, and in the end you took him in for me, Aunt Noriko."

Noriko was still looking down at her lap when her shoulders began to shake.

"And even more than that, you found my parents for me, before adopting me yourself. So how could I *not* be happy?"

So—you shouldn't be crying there, Noriko.

Instead of sobbing like that, it would be better to keep a

smile on your face till the end. And then I'm sure you'll be happier.

∽

Satoru began to stay overnight at the hospital more often.

"I'll be back in a few days."

He'd say this, tickle me on the head and leave the house, bag in hand. Gradually, the amount of time he stayed away grew longer. He'd say he'd be gone three or four days, but then would not come back for a week. Or he would say a week and return ten days later.

The clothes he had brought from Tokyo no longer fit him. His trousers became so loose you could fit a couple of fists inside the waist.

He started wearing a wool cap at home. I don't know why, but his hair was getting thinner than ever, along with his body, and then one day he was completely bald. I thought maybe they'd shaved his hair off at the hospital, but he'd gone to the barber's himself and got them to do it.

One day, as Satoru was preparing for another stay in the hospital, he put a photograph into his suitcase. A photo of the two of us, taken on one of our trips, which he'd always kept beside his bed back in Tokyo.

And then it struck me.

I stood up on my hind legs and scratched at my basket in

the corner of the living room and meowed. Come on, don't you need to bring this with you?

Satoru closed the clasp on his suitcase and smiled at me with a forlorn look.

"I guess you'd like to come with me, wouldn't you, Nana?"

Well, *of course*. Satoru opened the basket door, and I hurried inside. Then he turned the basket so the door was against the wall.

Just a second now! How am I supposed to get out? Enough with the silly jokes.

"You're very well behaved, so I know you'll be a good boy from now on."

Hold on there! I clawed hard at the inside of the basket. What're you talking about, Satoru?

Satoru stood up with his suitcase. He opened the front door without taking my basket with him.

Wait, wait! I scratched even harder at the basket, my fur on end, and yowled.

"I know you'll be a good boy."

Shut up—a *good boy*? What a load of hogwash! I'll never, ever let you leave me behind.

"You be a good boy now."

What? Come back here! Come back right this minute! *Take me with you!*

"It's not like I want to leave you. I love you, you silly cat!"

I love you, too, you dummy!

As if shaking off my yells, Satoru slowly left the room and closed the door firmly behind him.

Come back! Come back! *Come back!* COME BACK!

I'm your cat till the bitter end!

I screamed as loud as I could, but the door didn't open. I cried and cried and cried and cried, until my voice was completely hoarse.

After I'm not sure how long, when the room had turned dark, the door quietly clicked open.

It was Noriko. She moved my basket away from the wall and opened the door.

I stayed in the corner of the basket, sulking, and a small hand reached gingerly in.

With the tip of her finger she touched my head, scratched behind my ears, softly stroked my throat.

For someone who wasn't good with cats, she had come on quite well.

"Satoru said to take good care of you. Since you're his darling cat."

I know. That I'm precious to him—that much I know.

"I put out some food for you. I crumbled some chicken breast on top, too. Satoru said to pamper you today."

If he thinks that'll make up for leaving me behind, then he's got another thing coming.

"Satoru's room is kind of small, but it's a private room and very comfortable, not hospital-like at all. The nurses are all really kind, too. Satoru said he wants to spend his final days quietly."

Noriko's voice was trembling as she stroked me.

"So Satoru said to tell Nana not to worry at all."

Maybe I didn't need to worry, but without me there with him it must have been just awful.

"As soon as he got in the room he put up the photo of the two of you. Right next to his bed, just like at home. So he said everything's fine."

Nonsense. Which is better—a photo of me, or the real flesh-and-blood cat? The answer's obvious.

Of course having the real me there—warm and velvety-soft me—is better.

I licked Noriko's hand. At first, she hadn't liked it when I licked her; she said my tongue was rough.

Since you're crying, I'll eat later, when I feel so inclined. I mean, you went to all the trouble of topping it with chicken breast and all.

Other than eating and using the litter tray, I pretty much stayed holed up in Satoru's room.

Whenever I was alone in the house and the door opened, I leaped out, hoping it was him, but it was always Noriko.

I would let my tail droop and head back to Satoru's room. I wasn't at all embarrassed about letting it droop when I couldn't see him. Because it was only natural to feel sad.

It seemed that Satoru had asked Noriko to take me for a

walk every now and then, but if I couldn't go out with Satoru I didn't see the point of treading with the soft pads of my paws on streets covered with freezing white snow.

Satoru didn't seem to get it. How important he was to me.

Every day, I stared out of the window.

Hey, Satoru, how are things where you are?

There was an awful snowstorm today. A total white-out outside the window. I couldn't even see the lights of the city. Was it the same where you are?

Now it's sunny. Not a cloud in the sky. But the clear, blue sky looks really cold.

Today, the puffed-up sparrows on the power lines set a new record for rotundity. There are some thin clouds and it isn't snowing, but I'll bet it's freezing outside.

I saw a bright-red car driving down the road. The color of the berries on the mountain ash, the color you taught me. But I get the feeling the mountain-ash berry is a deeper color, the kind that takes your breath away. Humans are good at making colors, but they can't seem to reproduce the power of natural ones.

One day, Noriko walked into Satoru's room.

"Nana, let's go and visit Satoru."

Come again?

"Satoru seems really lonely without you, so I went ahead and asked if I could bring you. The doctor said you can't come inside, but when Satoru is going for his walk in the garden we can see him."

Bravo, Noriko!

Noriko held out the basket and I scurried inside. We drove there in the silver van. Noriko had been using it the whole time Satoru had been in hospital, apparently, and this was the first time I'd been in it since the last journey Satoru and I had taken together.

By car, it took all of twenty minutes.

Satoru was this close by.

If it were just me and Satoru in the van, I would have opened the basket instantly and slipped out, but since it was Noriko I stayed quietly inside. Unused to thinking about things from a cat's perspective, she put the basket on the floor in the back, so my only view was the van's dark interior.

"You stay here like a good boy, and I'll fetch Satoru."

As instructed, I waited like a good boy.

Of *course* I did. I'm a wise cat. I know what to do in any and all situations.

Finally, Noriko returned and lifted the basket out of the van.

The hospital was a tranquil place in a quiet neighborhood. Beyond the parking lot was a soft, snowy field. The trees and benches were decorated with a thick layer of snow. I imagined the grass and flowerbeds asleep underneath.

There were chairs and tables on a roofed-in terrace projecting out from the building, and this place seemed to be used as a rest area on days when the weather wasn't good. And then—

On the terrace, in a wheelchair, was Satoru.

I was impatient to leap out of the basket, but because Noriko was holding on to it, I refrained from unlocking the door myself.

"Nana!"

Satoru had a down jacket on and was all puffy, but he was even thinner and paler than the last time I'd seen him.

But then, a bit of color came to those ghostly cheeks. I don't think I'm being conceited if I say that I was the one who brought that warm red glow to his face, but what do you all think?

"I'm so glad you came!"

Satoru half rose from his wheelchair. Like me, he couldn't stand the distance still separating us. I wanted to open up the basket and leap straight out. But Noriko still didn't know I could unlock it myself.

I sprang into Satoru's lap as soon as I could.

He pressed me close in his thin arms, unable to speak. I purred till my throat hurt, rubbing the top of my head over and over against his body.

The two of us were so very, very well matched, so don't you think it was strange we were kept apart from each other?

I wanted to lie in his arms forever, but pretty soon the piercing cold became too much for Satoru, in his condition.

"Satoru," Noriko said hesitantly. Satoru knew what she meant, but found it hard to let me go.

"I keep the photo of the two of us next to my bed."

Um. Noriko told me.

"So I'm not lonely."

That's not true. In fact, it's such an obvious lie that Enma, the Lord of Hell, who pulls out the tongues of liars, would be laughing too hard to do any tongue-pulling.

"You stay well, Nana."

One more firm squeeze around my middle that nearly brought the stuffing out of me, and Satoru finally let me go. At Noriko's urging, I stepped straight back into my basket, ever the good boy.

"Just a second. I'll put Nana in the car."

Noriko left me on the backseat of the van before hurrying back to Satoru.

That was my moment. With my right paw, I flipped the basket door open. I sat down low in the driver's seat and waited for Noriko to return.

It was almost an hour later when she did. There was a light dusting of snow swirling in the air, and Noriko was hunching up her shoulders against the cold as she walked.

The door on the driver's side snapped open.

"Nana?!"

She chased after me, but when it comes to playing tag, humans are no match for four-legged animals. I avoided her easily and raced out into the parking lot.

"Come back here!"

Noriko's voice was nearly a scream. Sorry, but I'm not going to listen to you.

Because I'm a wise cat, who knows what to do in any and all situations.

When I had reached a safe distance, I stopped and turned to look, focusing my vision hard on her flailing, distant figure.

Then I put up my tail cheerily.

See you! Bye!

I scampered off into the snowy landscape and never looked back.

∽

Now then. No matter how proud a stray cat I might be, winter in Hokkaido is pretty formidable.

The snow in Tokyo should never be called by the same name as the snow that falls here, so heavy sometimes you can't see your nose in front of your face.

Here's where all those walks I'd taken with Satoru came in useful.

The town cats I ran across were great at slipping into sheltered spaces to avoid the cold. And, of course, there were some heroic cats in the neighborhood around the hospital as well.

That being the case, since I was always prepared to go back to being a stray, why wouldn't I survive?

Using the hospital as my base, I located several spots where I could keep out of the cold. As might be expected with large buildings, there were many cracks and gaps—in garage and warehouse walls, for instance—that a cat could slip through. The areas below the flooring in people's houses and underneath their boilers were both comfortable places. Sometimes, another cat had beaten me to it, but perhaps the severe winter cold helped foster a spirit of cooperation, and more often than not we would end up sharing the spot rather than disputing it.

I'd heard that the citizens of Hokkaido were particularly kind. Noriko had told Satoru that it was quite common for people to pick up drunks and travelers and let them stay in their home. Sure enough, I experienced how that principle operated in the cat world, too.

The local cats showed me where to scavenge for food, for example. Houses and shops where they'd give you tasty leftovers, and a park where a cat lover might feed you. There was a small supermarket near the hospital as well, and I often charmed my way into cadging treats there.

And, of course, there was always hunting. The cold made the puffed-up birds and mice move nice and slowly, so they were easy prey.

The cats around me thought I was a little odd for having intentionally given up the easy life for one as a stray. *Why do that?* they often asked. *It's such a waste.* They concluded I must be a little mad.

But, for me, there was something more important at stake.

The snow began to let up, and night was yet to fall. I crept around to the side of the warehouse from which the hospital was visible and—yes! Just as I thought.

Satoru, wheeling himself in his wheelchair, was coming out of the front door.

Tail straight up, I scampered over to him. His face broke into a tearful smile. Then he said, "You need to go home now."

You know what'll happen if you try to catch me, don't you? I'll scratch you—up and down and all over—until you look like they could play checkers on your face.

Satoru could see I was wary, and said, "I give up."

Turns out, when I escaped from Noriko, they had totally freaked out. Satoru was apparently so shocked when he heard I'd run away he broke out in a fever.

Noriko looked for me every day on the streets but, naturally, I was too stealthy for the likes of her to find me.

A few days passed, and when I turned up again in front of Satoru, despondently sitting on the terrace, boy was he surprised! His jaw dropped so far he looked like Donald Duck.

See? Didn't I tell you I'd stay with you to the end?

Satoru reached out from his wheelchair to grab me. I flailed around like a freshly caught salmon and slipped out of his grasp.

When I looked up at him from a safe spot on the floor a few yards away, Satoru's face looked like that of a child on the verge of tears.

"Nana, you're being foolish," he said. "You came to say hello, didn't you?"

I am Satoru's one and only cat. And Satoru is my one and only pal.

And a proud cat like me wasn't about to abandon his pal. If living as a stray was what it took to be Satoru's cat to the very end, then bring it on.

When Noriko heard the news from Satoru, she huffed and puffed and jumped in her car. I'm not sure where she found it, but she brought over a huge cage used to trap animals, left it in the garage and went back home. As if I would be stupid enough to get caught in a contraption like that!

For a while, I couldn't trust the hospital staff either. Apparently acting on instructions from Noriko and Satoru, they tried to coax me over, with the sole intention of capturing me.

They saw me appear whenever Satoru happened to be on the terrace, only to leave as soon as he went inside, so I think they finally understood.

After that, I became Satoru's commuting cat.

On days when it wasn't snowing, Satoru would come outside for a short while, and we'd spend some precious moments together. I chewed on the crunchies and chicken breast he brought me and curled up tightly in his lap.

Satoru would tickle me behind my ears and under my chin, and I'd purr for him.

Just like when we first met.

M r. Miyawaki?"
　　　　The nurse was calling him back inside. She was about the same age as Noriko, but quite a bit rounder.

"Okay. I'll be in soon."

Satoru held me tightly to his body. Whenever we parted, he would always give me a huge hug. I could tell from the way his thin arms clung around me that this might be the last time.

I licked Satoru's hands, each and every knuckle, and leaped down from his lap.

B y the way, when I became a commuting cat, some of the other cats I got to know received extra perks as well.

The hospital staff and visitors started to leave little snacks around the yard for me. Each one thought they were the only one stealthily leaving me food, but actually there must have been a whole lot of them.

I couldn't eat it all myself, but took some to all the cats who'd been kind to me, to repay them.

I t snowed for several days in a row.

When it finally let up, I sidled over to the side of the warehouse where I had a clear view of the hospital's front entrance.

It was the first sunny day in a while, yet Satoru didn't appear on the terrace.

When the sun began to set, Noriko pulled up in the silver van. Her face looked pale, her hair disheveled.

I pattered up to her, but she said simply, "Sorry, Nana. You'll have to wait," and walked swiftly inside.

༽

I n the hospital room, all Noriko could do was watch.

The waves on the ECG machine were getting steadily weaker.

She could just see the figure of Satoru lying on the bed, between the members of staff clustered around him.

As Noriko tried to slide between them, a nurse brushed against the bedside cabinet and two framed photos—a family photo with Noriko, and one of Nana—fell crashing to the floor. They were hurriedly retrieved and put back in place.

Just then, a cat's mewling from outside resounded around the ward. Mewling and mewling.

"Can I—"

Noriko spoke before thinking.

"Can I bring in the cat? Satoru's cat?"

She'd never made such an absurd request in her life.

"Please—let me bring in the cat."

"Please don't ask!" the matron scolded. "If you ask, then we'll have to say no!"

As if propelled by a cannon, Noriko raced out of the ward. Ignoring the No Running in the Corridor sign, she clattered down the stairs, two at a time.

Then she burst through the front entrance.

"Nana! *Naaana!*"

Nana leaped out of the darkness like a silver bullet. He

jumped into Noriko's arms and snuggled into her body. Then Noriko raced back up to the ward.

"Satoru!"

The staff were reaching the final stages of the procedure. Noriko elbowed her way through them to Satoru's side.

"Satoru, it's Nana!"

Satoru's closed eyelids quivered. As if fighting against gravity, they slowly lifted.

Unable to move his head, his eyes searched from side to side.

Noriko clasped Satoru's hand and placed it gently on the top of Nana's small head.

Satoru's lips moved faintly. She thought she heard him say, "Thank you."

The ECG screen flat-lined.

Nana nuzzled the top of his head up and down against Satoru's lifeless hand.

"I'm afraid he's passed away," the attending doctor said, and the matron added, "We can't have you bringing a cat in here. You'll have to take him out now."

Suddenly, the atmosphere seemed to lighten. Some of the nurses even gave a small smile.

And then, as though something loose had finally been wrenched open, the floodgates broke.

Not since she was a little girl had Noriko wept with such abandon.

The staff members finished unplugging the monitors and took them away.

"Make sure you take the cat outside immediately," the matron reminded her, before swiftly leaving the room.

Noriko's throat throbbed, until she couldn't weep anymore.

Suddenly, she felt a rough tongue licking the tops of her fingers. Gently, ever so gently.

"Let's take Satoru back, Nana."

As if in response, Nana licked her hand again.

"Nana, is it okay for me to believe that Satoru was happy?"

Nana nuzzled his forehead against Noriko's palm, and then once more began to lick, ever so delicately.

Not the End of the Road

Purple and yellow flowers in bloom as far as the eye can see.

The earthy, warm colors of Hokkaido in autumn.

There I am, chasing a honeybee.

Stop it, Nana.

A voice sounding flustered. He grabs hold of me and carries me tightly in his two hands.

What if you get stung?

Satoru, smiling as he reprimands me.

Hey, it's been a while. You look good.

I rub my small cheeks against Satoru's arms.

All thanks to you. How about you, Nana?

I'm good—all thanks to you.

Ever since the day he departed on his journey, every time Satoru visits me it's always in this field. This open expanse, with its riot of flowers.

But I wonder how many more of these winters I can put up with.

You're getting on.

Don't say that. Just because you left this world when you were younger than me, don't get carried away.

A mellow sun shines but there is a dusting of snow fluttering in the air. Another winter is just around the corner.

And I'm finally coming to the end of my story.

Satoru left behind a list of people he was close to or who had helped him in one way or another, together with a note requesting that they all be contacted and thanked. Which Noriko duly did.

I was amazed by how many condolence letters and telegrams flooded in. Not just from friends, but from colleagues and former supervisors at work, and even from former school teachers of his. Even people Noriko didn't contact, but who had heard the news, got in touch.

Noriko was terribly busy dealing with them all. I think it was good for her to be busy so soon after Satoru passed away. I was worried she would become depressed after his death. "She might age a whole decade," Satoru told me when he was in hospital. "So you've got to stay by her side, okay?"

In the end, Noriko aged maybe two or three years, max. I mean, she wasn't that young to begin with (about as old as Momo the cat, I imagine), so a couple of years wasn't going to make much difference. Oops. If Noriko or Momo heard that, I imagine they'd be pretty upset!

"Satoru knew so many kind and thoughtful people, Nana."

As well as sending their condolences, people asked to come

and light incense and pray in memory of him. They were all people I knew, and Satoru had left handwritten letters for all of them.

On Honshu, the main island, the cherry blossoms were blooming further and further northward. They wouldn't start blooming in Hokkaido for a while, though. On the streets of Sapporo, there was even some leftover snow in the shadier spots.

The weather was dodgy for a few days, but on the day of the funeral the sun shone. It was as though Satoru was welcoming his guests. It was a quiet affair, with only Noriko and relatives on his mother's side attending. I waited at home while the funeral was taking place. I can't say I'm much interested in the ceremonies humans like to conduct.

I was in the hospital to see him off. But he's still here, in my heart, so I don't need a ceremony to remember him.

Later, several people I hadn't seen for a long time arrived at Noriko's and my apartment: Kosuke and Yoshimine, and Sugi and Chikako.

They all wore black and didn't say much, their lips drawn.

"Please—come on in. I ordered some sushi. It's fine to have some, now that the period of abstinence is over. And I'll make some soup to go with it, so please wait a moment."

Noriko said this cheerfully, but the others were concerned they were causing too much trouble.

"I'm so sorry you have to do all this," Kosuke said, and all the other guests murmured their agreement, bowing to her.

"Don't worry about it. I'm delighted to have Satoru's friends over."

"Do you need some help?" Chikako said, standing up. But Noriko waved her offer away.

"Don't worry. I'm really not comfortable having people in my kitchen."

As usual, Noriko didn't mean anything by this, but it made Chikako feel a little awkward. If Satoru had been there, he would have said, "I'm sorry. Her heart's in the right place." But Noriko kept her eyes fixed on the chopping board and didn't seem to notice.

If she had seen Chikako's reaction, she would no doubt have said something else and dug herself into an even deeper hole.

"Instead of helping, why don't you play with Nana?"

Oh—well played, Noriko, to get me in on the act. I went over to Chikako and rubbed the side of my body up against her leg.

"Hi, Nana. I wish we could have taken you in," she said, reaching down to fondle my tummy.

"Hm?" Kosuke said. "Did Satoru arrange a meeting with Nana for you, too?"

"He did," said Chikako and Sugi together, both smiling wryly. "Our dog and Nana didn't really get on, so it didn't work out."

"For me, it was my kitten that was the problem." This from Yoshimine.

This seemed to break the ice, and they all started telling each other their Nana stories. "Nana is surprisingly fussy," Kosuke said. An uncalled-for remark, if you ask me.

Oh, really? And who's the one who quarrels with his wife and gets all weepy about it, eh?

It seemed that Kosuke and his wife had adopted their own cat. Kosuke proudly showed a few photos on his phone of a pretty silver mackerel tabby. You and Satoru might have been childhood friends, but there's no need to show off your cat like that.

Then Yoshimine pulled out his mobile phone. "Me too," he said, passing it around.

Et tu, Yoshimine? That cat with the silly name, Chatran, had grown up to be a rugged young thing. He was an expert at catching mice now. Perhaps my efforts to train him had paid off.

"Satoru met him, so I thought I'd show him this photo."

Yoshimine got up and went over to the altar in the corner of the room set up in memory of Satoru.

"If I'd known we were going to be bragging about our pets, I would have brought my photo album," Chikako said, but she and Sugi weren't about to be left behind when it came to animal photos. Both of them pulled out their mobile phones to share photos of Momo and Toramaru.

"We run a bed and breakfast that welcomes pets, so please

stop by sometime," Sugi said, pulling out some business cards. They all exchanged addresses.

You know something, Satoru? After you passed away, the people who miss you all became connected.

"If you wouldn't mind taking one, too?" Sugi said to Noriko, handing her his business card as she brought in the sushi.

Yes, please, give her one, I thought. I'd like to lie down all snug on top of that boxy warm TV set again someday.

"Thanks. I haven't climbed Mount Fuji in ages, and that would be lovely."

Go right ahead, Noriko. I'll hold the fort back at the Sugis', on top of that toasty TV.

They all sat around the table, eagerly sharing stories about Satoru.

"What? So Satoru didn't swim in junior high?" Kosuke blinked in surprise.

"That's right." Yoshimine nodded. "When he was with me, we were in the gardening club together. Was he that good at swimming?"

"He was in the swimming club all through elementary school. He won a lot of races in big galas, and people had high hopes for him ... Did he swim in high school?"

Sugi and Chikako both shook their heads.

"He had a lot of friends, but he wasn't in any particular club."

"Really? He was such a fast swimmer. I wonder why he gave it up."

As she gave me some tuna sushi, minus the wasabi, Noriko casually murmured, "Must have been because you were no longer with him, Kosuke."

Oh, Noriko, what is *wrong* with you? You're usually so clumsy with words, but occasionally what you say is spot-on and cuts right to the quick. Kosuke's face fell.

"As he was writing those letters, he told me a lot about all of you. About how he and you, Kosuke, ran away from home with the cat, and that he was a little bit worried about you since you and your wife had argued."

Come on now—you didn't have to say that!

"We're fine now," Kosuke hurriedly explained.

"He told me how much he enjoyed helping you, Yoshimine, and your grandmother in the fields, and how you always did things at your own pace and ran off in the middle of class to take care of the greenhouse, and how anxious that made him."

Yoshimine looked out of the window, as if deep in thought.

"He also told me how Sugi and Chikako loved animals and were a great couple together, and how happy he was when he got to see you again in college."

Kosuke's bottom lip began to tremble, and Chikako wiped away tears.

"But why . . ." Sugi muttered. "Why didn't Satoru tell us he was sick?"

That's disappointing. Just like always, you stammer out things you shouldn't.

You really don't understand why?

"I kind of understand why," Yoshimine said. "He wanted to say farewell with everybody still smiling."

Bingo!

Satoru loved all of you guys.

That's why he wanted to take your smiles with him.

Simple enough, I think.

"The letters ..." Kosuke's voice was weepy, but he smiled all the same. "In his letters, he wrote about all kinds of funny things. Silly jokes and gags, too. I laughed, thinking, This can't be his last letter, can it?"

They all chuckled.

When it was time for them to leave, Noriko drove them to the airport in the silver van. Satoru's silver van had become Noriko's silver van. Though no longer the magical vehicle that had shown Satoru and me so many amazing sights, it still did the job.

Okay, then. Before Noriko got back, I had something to do.

Noriko came home after dark, and as she wandered into the living room she let out a scream.

"EEEEK! Nana! You did it again!"

I'd removed every single tissue from the box and was sitting quietly in the corner contemplating the result of my actions.

"You don't use them, so why take them out?"

Good point. But as you focus on your anger and on tidying up the floor, don't all your sad feelings begin to lift a bit?

"What a waste! What a complete waste!" Noriko muttered as she strutted around picking up the tissues, but then, as if letting out a soft puff of air, she laughed.

∽

Several years have passed.

Kosuke turned his shop into a studio specializing in pet photos. This was thanks to Satoru's advice, he told us, so I was welcome anytime for a free photo session. But the New Year cards that arrive have begun to feature bizarre photos of his dressed-up mackerel tabby, who always looks so sullen. So I'll take a rain check.

Now and again, Yoshimine sends us vegetables he's grown. *I'm sure Hokkaido has great vegetables, too*, he writes in the short note he always includes in his vegetable box. It's more than Noriko could eat by herself, so she's kept busy running around, sharing them all out with her friends and acquaintances.

Noriko did take me once to stay at the Sugis' B&B. The purpose, though, was for her to climb Mount Fuji while the Sugis took care of me. While she was gone, I enjoyed the warmth of that boxy TV underneath my belly to my heart's content.

Momo had become a refined old lady cat, and nervy Tora-maru had transformed into quite the sensible pooch. Sorry about back then, he apologized.

I almost forgot—the Sugis have a child now. A precocious little girl who greeted Noriko with a "Welcome, Grandma," which made her blush.

The berries on the mountain ash along the streets are bright red again this year. And pretty soon there'll be a constant layer of snow on the ground.

How many times, I wonder, have I seen this red that Satoru taught me?

One day, Noriko brought home a very unexpected guest.

"What should I do, Nana?"

A siren-like wail was coming from the cardboard box she was carrying. Inside was a calico kitten. Not an *almost*-calico, but a genuine one. And because it was a pure calico, it was, of course, a female.

"Someone abandoned it under the apartment building. I thought, since you're already here, Nana ..."

I sniffed at the wailing siren and gently gave it a lick under its chin.

Welcome. You're the next cat, aren't you?

"We're just back from the vet. Nana, do you think you two will get on?"

Save that for later. Right now, you've got to get some milk into its tummy. The little gal seems hungry.

I got into the box and snuggled close to the little creature to warm it up, and she promptly tried to find some nipples on me. Sorry, sweetheart—no milk to be had here.

"Oh, she's hungry, isn't she? I've bought some milk for her. Let me warm it up."

And so Noriko plunged into a life in which this demanding young kitten has her wrapped around her little finger every single day.

∽

P urple and yellow like a flood.

The field I saw on our last journey, bursting all the way to the horizon with flowers.

When I dream about these colors, Satoru always appears.

Hey, Nana. How have you been? Aren't you a little worn out?

I suppose so. Momo at the Sugis' left us a few years ago. I might not last as long as she did. And we have a new cat that's arrived to take over.

Is Aunt Noriko doing okay?

Having that kitten seems to have put a spring in her step.

Noriko named the kitten Calico, after her looks. When it comes to giving the most obvious, second-rate names, you and Noriko are like two peas in a pod, I must say.

Really? It's hard to think that she'd take in a stray cat.

Satoru seems genuinely moved.

Surprisingly, she has the makings of a cat fanatic. Whenever she gets sushi, she always gives me the *toro*, the best part of the tuna.

Even I might have trouble handing over the *toro*, Satoru says, laughing.

This is the first cat of her own she's ever had.

That's right.

We live together, but I'm not Noriko's cat.

Forever and ever I am your cat, Satoru. That's why I can't become Noriko's.

So, about time, maybe, for you to come over here?

Yeah, but I have one more thing I need to do first.

Satoru looks puzzled. Ahem, I say, and twitch my whiskers.

I have to help little Calico get on her feet. Noriko isn't training her at all.

If she becomes too spoiled and ever tries to make it on her own on the streets, she'll be toast. At the very least, I've got to hammer the basics of hunting into her.

To be fair, when you grab her by the scruff of the neck, her legs do immediately contract, so she clearly has potential. Much more than, say, Chatran at Yoshimine's.

Once Calico can make it on her own, I think I'll set off on my journey. To this place I see only in dreams.

Tell me, Satoru. What's out there beyond this field? A lot of wonderful things, I'm thinking. I wonder if I'll be able to go on a trip with you again.

Satoru grins, and picks me up, so I can see the far-off horizon from his eye level.

Ah—we saw so many things, didn't we?

· ·

M y story will be over soon.
But it's not something to be sad about.

As we count up the memories from one journey, we head off on another.

Remembering those who went ahead. Remembering those who will follow after.

And someday, we will meet all those people again, out beyond the horizon.